Biggest Regret

First Edition: April 2025

Editor: Alexandra McLaughlin

Cover Design by: crimsonsdesigns

979-8-9927247-07 (Trade paperback)

979-8-9927247-1-4 (ebook)

Biggest Regret

DWYM Series Book Two

Amaia Denise

AUTHOR NOTES

This story is a continuation of Lily and Jace from *Biggest Fan*. While I intended each book in this series to hold on its own, it is important to note that this book contains **major spoilers** for *Biggest Fan*. **Read at your own risk.**

As known from *Biggest Fan*, Jace is Irish and switches back and forth with his accent and language. Throughout this story, he does throw in a ton of Irish language. I did as much research as I could since I find it to be a beautiful language, but I would like to apologize in advance for any miscommunication.

I thank each and every one of you who decided to continue following the *Do What You Must* series. I hope you fall in love with Jace as much as I did.

Love forever,

A.D.

Instagram: @authoramaia

TikTok: @authoramaiadenise

TRIGGER WARNINGS

This book contains content that might be troubling to some readers, including, but not limited to, suicide, stalking, murder, sexual assault, gun play, breath play, downgrading, kidnapping, sex trafficking, and substance use and abuse. It contains sexually explicit material and scenes meant for mature adult readers (18+).
If any of these content warnings may be a trigger for you as a reader, **please do not proceed.**

PLAYLIST

Scan a QR code to listen:

<table>
<tr><td align="center">SPOTIFY</td><td align="center">APPLE MUSIC</td></tr>
<tr><td align="center"></td><td align="center"></td></tr>
</table>

Part 1

“Boulevard of Broken Dreams” by: Green Day
“Breakin’ Dishes” by: Rihanna
“Duality” by: Slipknot
“Howlin’ for You” by: The Black Keys
“Bad Intentions (Feat. Migos)” by: Niykee Heaton
“Human” by: Sevdaliza
“Awkward” by: SZA
“Blind” by: Korn
“Don’t Hurt Yourself (Feat. Jack White)” by: Beyoncé
“Sex on Fire” by: Kings of Leon
“Stupid Girl” by: Garbage
“Something in the Way” by: Nirvana
“I Hate Everything About You” by: Three Days Grace
“Glory Box” by: Portishead
“I Wanna Be Yours” by: Artic Monkeys
“Twist” by: Korn

"Breathin" by: Ariana Grande
Part 2
"No Good" by: Roux
"Save the World" by: We Are Not Friends & Nextime
"Favorite Part" by: Sabrina Claudio
"Bad At Love" by: Halsey
"Aphrodite" by: Sam Short
"No One Knows" by: Queen of the Stone Age
"Bad Influence" by: P!nk
"Touchin' Me" by: Chandler Leighton
"Cherry Waves" by: Deftones
"Underneath It All (Feat Lady Shaw)" by: No Doubt
"Bring Me to Life" by: Evanescence
"Nothing Else Matters" by: Metallica
"Lonely Day" by: System of A Down
"Me and Your Mama (Mixed)" by: Childish Gambino
"icantbelieveiletyougetaway" by: aldn
"listen before i go" by: Billie Eilish
"Carry Me Home (feat. Maverick Sabre)" by: Jorja Smith
"Running Up That Hill (A Deal With God) [Piano Version]"
by: Henry Smith
"Nothing Sweeter" by: Naomi Sharon

PROLOGUE

Jace

I sit next to Rowan in Club Opal, drumming my fingers against my knee in sync with my heart pounding against my chest. I feel the cold leather couch seep through my jeans, creating goosebumps along my skin.

"Start from the beginning. I want everything." This is my second time asking, but I don't care. It doesn't make sense. His story is not processing in my brain.

I feel Rowan's weight lifted off the couch and I let my head fall into my hands, peeking through my fingers to see his feet disappear out of the VIP room. I stare at the red carpet that Axel installed. I told him to go black, but he felt that red was a better color for business. I met Axel, the owner of Club Opal, while I was disposing of a body in a *schuch* years ago. Apparently, the land I was using was his, which made sense why, when I was digging my holes, I kept finding bodies that I had not put there myself. We ended up chit-chatting, and he told me about this club he planned on opening. He said he would discount Rowan's and my membership if we coordinated our business with his.

I lift my head from my hands when I hear the VIP curtains rip open. Rowan walks back in with a bottle in his hand and dips down onto the couch. "I got a call from Lance. He told me to come to the house. By the time I got there, there were cops surrounding the place. Lance told the officer that she hasn't been home in three days." Rowan takes off the bourbon cap, shrugging his shoulders and taking a sip of the whiskey.

We have known each other since we were children. We went to school together, fought together, at one point even lived together. Our lives weren't like the other children's growing up. Yes, Rowan came from old money, but he wasn't treated like the other kids who grew up with money, nor did he act like it. He used to come to school bruised and beaten. Nobody seemed to care except me.

I glance at the kid sitting beside me. I read the name tag placed on his desk. I recognize that name on the large building I walk past every morning on my way to school. My eyes roam from his name tag to his ripped jeans and long-sleeve shirt. He has scattered bruises and cuts along his fingers and ankles. His black hair covers most of his face as he leans into his arms, coloring on his desk.

The bell rings and I see all the kids get out of their seats, heading to the door to leave for recess. The only kids who have not moved are me and Rowan. I see his hand scribbling faster on the desk.

"Can I see?" I ask. Rowan turns his head over his shoulder to look at me.

I remember that day like it was fucking yesterday. Young Rowan with a busted lip and black eye. Now, he's labeled New York's most eligible billionaire in multiple magazines.

"And Lance doesn't know where she fucking went? He keeps track of her like she is a dog," I snap.

Rowan leans back on the couch, taking another gulp of the now half-empty bottle. Joan Harper went missing tonight. Gone without a word, without a trace. Rowan's mother was everything to him. *To us.* I can't sit back and wait for the police to pretend to do their job. For Lance to pretend to care about his wife.

Chapter One

Lily

Three Years Later…

♫ "Boulevard of Broken Dreams" - Green Day ♫

I swear, if this stupid keyboard goes out one more time, I'm tossing it out the window. I look at my bedroom window, remembering it is nailed shut. Okay, never mind.

I hang my head over my desk chair, staring at my ceiling while spinning in a circle. I have a test due in two hours. I haven't eaten since… oh I don't know, yesterday? I have notes scattered along my desk, and I can't see the floor in my room due to all the open books. Every time I turn on my computer it gives me some type of matrix coded program, as if I'm some kind of computer wizard. I continue to distract myself by counting the number of holes I have on my ceiling. It should only take a couple of minutes before my screen is back up and running.

I stop spinning my chair when I hear the doorbell ring. I tap my phone screen to see it's 10 a.m. I shake my head, getting out of my chair. The only person who could be ringing the doorbell at 10 a.m. is none other than my best friend, Celeste, who I will be murdering for running away last night to go make up with her boyfriend and not tell me. I mean, I did tell her to go kiss and make up, but she could have told me *she was going to go kiss and make up*, instead of having me sit at home all night worrying my ass off.

"Forget your keys, did you?" I shout while walking to the door. I unlatch and unlock all the deadbolts I installed and swing the door open. I squeeze my eyebrows together, putting my hands on my hips. "What are you doing here?"

I thought it was Celeste at the door because she left her keys, but no, fucking Jace is standing in front of me looking like a deer in the headlights. I watch his eyes dart from my legs to my face, then look back over his shoulder. I scan my own body, noticing I am only wearing boyshort underwear and a tight tank top my breasts are overflowing out of. I've worn this exact equal amount of clothing in the club, so I don't know why his cheeks are flaming red as if he has never seen me like this before. I slam the door in his face since he is taking too long to answer my question.

"*Álainn*, I need you to open the door."

"No thanks. You have the wrong house!" I yell through the door.

"Lily. Open. The door."

I place my ear to the cold wooden frame. "Why?"

"It's about Celeste."

I open the door, peeking my head out. "What happened? Where is she? I swear, if you guys killed her, I will murder you and your entire family. I watch murder documentaries. I know how to get rid of a body. All you need is—" Jace shoves the door open, forcing my body into the foyer table. "Hey! Excuse you! I did not say you can come in!" I kick my front door shut and follow him down the hallway and into my kitchen. He sets his laptop on the counter and drops a duffle bag on the floor.

Oh lord, he is here to murder me.

"Look, I don't have any money. I doubt Celeste hides money in the house. I mean, Jesus, I'm in college and we live in New York. If you plan on robbing and killing someone, I suggest you head upstate to the rich folks," I propose, but instead of him responding to me, he lets this eerie undeclared silence waft between us—and oh. My. God. Why is he staring at me like that? I shake my head, lift my hands to my sides, and let them slap against my thighs. "Are you going to answer me?!"

His throat bobs and his eyes dart around the room. "I'm here to watch ya and I need you to go pack some clothes for Celeste."

"Why? Where is she?"

"Eh, well—" He rubs the back of his head and my eyes clock his curled biceps. "Celeste and Rowan are going on an emergency trip, and Rowan told me to be here with you. I've got a lad coming to grab her bag in ten, so if you can hurry along, that will be helpful."

"If they are only going on a trip then why do you need to be here?" I cross my arms over my chest and his eyes go wide as he looks from my chest back to my face. What I am wearing is probably frying his brain. Maybe that's why he can't answer any of my questions properly. I huff, turning around to go to my room and find some clothes.

"Why did Rowan tell you to come be with me? I don't need a babysitter just because my friend is going on a little romantic getaway!" I scream from my bedroom. I start throwing clothes out of my dresser, trying to find something decent to wear. After nearly emptying out my drawers, I find old grey sweatpants and an equally old band T-shirt. I quickly throw them on and walk out of my room to stand in front of Jace again.

"*Álainn*, please just go pack Celeste some clothes."

I squint my eyes, studying him as I tap my foot on the floor. I should kick him out. What if this is all a setup? What if he is lying? What if Celeste is not okay, there is no romantic getaway, and he is here to do bad things to me? Or something. If he thinks he can just barge in here and tell me what to do, well… then he has the wrong woman. If this is true and Celeste is going on a trip with Rowan, well then sorry, Celeste, but I am not going to deal with this while you two get to play husband and wife. I am standing my ground. Putting my foot down.

I place my hands on my hips, raise one eyebrow, and tap my foot on the ground like my mother use to do to me when I was in trouble. Jace takes a seat on the bar stool and crosses his arms over his chest. His piercing blue eyes fix on me and my green eyes fix on him. His blank, emotionless face is making me slightly uncomfortable, but I let minutes pass by as we both stand in our places, staring at each other. I don't even know how this will change the situation. Either way, Celeste is leaving, and I can only blame myself. If my drunk ass hadn't let Rowan in our house the morning after the club, Celeste wouldn't be going on this getaway slash emergency trip.

I drop my hands off my hips, giving up. "Fine." I stomp into her room, opening her closet. If she is going on this trip, then I am packing all the outfits she never wears—her dresses, her lingerie, even all the cute tops that I gave her from my closet, and because I am a great friend, I will give her *one* outfit that she will feel comfortable in: jeans and a T-shirt.

I shove it all into a duffle bag and drag it over to where Jace is sitting and typing at the speed of lightning on his laptop. "How long are they going to be gone for?" I ask.

"I don't know."

"Well... Where are they going?"

"Can't tell ya," he says, his eyes glued to the laptop screen.

"Why not 'aye'?" I mock his accent, but my smile gradually falls when he stops typing and the air becomes a little too thick. He turns on the bar stool, facing me. His jaw clenches as his eyes search into my soul. I look down toward the duffle bag at his feet that he brought with him. Chills crawl over my skin at the thought of only weapons being in there. I've heard what Rowan and Jace do for work and I have to admit, it's pretty intimating, and how could I forget what happened to that man in Athens? I mean, Rowan did have the right to kill him since he was trying to hurt Celeste, but I think about how he was found days later, shoved into a closet, missing multiple limbs, and I'm afraid I might be next.

I rock back and forth on my feet, rolling the hem of my T-shirt between my fingers. "Forget it. I will call her myself." I start walking away to my room, but I'm yanked back by my arm, my head snapping into Jace's chest. I wrap my hand around his bicep for stability as his face is only inches away from mine. This is it. He is going to kill me. I am going to be shoved into a closet with missing limbs and who knows when Celeste will find me.

"Don't. Do. That. Again," he says behind his teeth as I feel his thumb draw circles on my arms. His grip goes from deadly to friendly as he adds, "Your voice is too pretty to mock my accent, *álainn.*" I can see his irises expand as they scan my face.

I've never seen eyes as blue as his. They are not blue with multiple shades, no, his eyes are pure blue, like the sky on a clear day. Freckles dot around his face, giving him a bronzy glow and god, his— I move my hands from his biceps to his chest and push him off me. I turn on my heels, walk back to my room, and slam my door shut. I pick up my phone from my desk, clicking Celeste's contact. I stand there listening to the line ring until it goes to voicemail.

"Bitch, I swear to god, if you are not already dead, I am going to murder you myself." I pause and think about how she could possibly already be dead. "I'm sorry. I take that back. I won't murder you. Please just call me back." I hang up the phone and stare at my screen, waiting for a text or a call back.

Nothing.

I throw my phone on my bed, turning to look at my computer to see it's finally not in the *Matrix*, and turn to the clock to see I now have only an hour to submit this test. My professor gave us this test a week ago, but due to me working two jobs and having half my classes online and half in person, I waited until the last minute to submit. This test is supposed to prepare us for our civil procedure final, but the only thing I feel like it is preparing me for is my death.

Nobody knows that I barely made it into NYU Law by the tips of my fingernails. I'm smart, but for whatever reason, I freak out when it comes to exams, tests, and anything that could put my future at risk.

Throughout high school, I took specific courses to help me with test anxiety, but it didn't remove the pressure build up I get in my chest anytime I read the first page.

Multiple choice tests tend to be easy for me. When I don't know the answer, I automatically pick B or C. Everybody knows one of those options is always the correct answer. But when we get to written tests, my stomach swirls and bubbles, making me want to vomit all my organs. All this unnecessary stress just to receive a law degree that I don't want.

When I was a kid, I used to play judge with my father. I would put on my mother's robe and run around the house with a wooden spoon, banging it on furniture and screaming, "Court in order!" That was over twenty years ago, and when I turned eighteen and told my parents I was moving to the States for college, their eyes lit up like the Fourth of July. They failed to catch my facial expression or my denial when they started chanting that their daughter was going to be an attorney.

They held on to that little girl who wanted to be responsible for delivering justice and that same little girl couldn't be responsible for their heartbreak when she told them that was not what she wanted. So here I am, five years later, unable to keep my sanity, unable to keep my room clean, working two jobs, discarding and piling outfit drawings into my desk drawer, and lying to my parents when they call.

Chapter Two

Lily

♫ "Breakin' Dishes" - Rihanna ♫

I grab my stomach when I hear it rumble, warning me it will eat me alive if I don't feed it. It took me an extra two hours to finish my test, which means it was late, and I will probably receive a failing grade. But at least I finished.

I walk out of my room, heading to the kitchen, but my quest to feed myself is suspended when I see Jace sitting on my couch. I had completely forgotten I have a stranger in my house. I should try to make him leave again. Force him out. Threaten him out, but my tummy says to wait, so I head toward the fridge, leaning my head inside to see only mayonnaise, bread, butter, ketchup, and milk.

Great.

"I ordered us pizza."

I flinch, my head hitting the top of the fridge. "Mother fu—" I turn around, rubbing at the top of my head to see Jace standing right behind me. "Announce yourself before you end up giving someone a heart attack."

"My apologies."

I wish I could smack those freckles right off his face. He is wearing dark-wash jeans and a white T-shirt tight enough to see the outline of his abs. I roll my eyes and walk past him to go into the living room. I turn on the TV and sit on the couch, and for a fraction of a moment, I think about asking him what he wants to watch, but then I remember this is my house and he is practically trespassing—so I turn the TV on to *True Blood*. I turn my head toward the hallway when I hear the front door slam shut, Jace coming around the corner with four boxes of pizza in his hands.

"Why so many?" I ask.

He shrugs his shoulders as he drops the boxes on the coffee table. "I didn't know what you liked."

He opens the top of the pizza box. Pineapple and ham. "Um. Ew."

"Don't knock it until ya try it," he says as he grabs a slice and winks at me. He sits down on the couch only inches away and swings his arm to rest above my head.

I scoot away from him to try and avoid any physical contact. *"Don't knock it until ya try it."* I've heard him speak without an accent. He can turn it on and off like a switch.

Which is completely and utterly annoying. Either be yourself or don't.

I glance to my right, seeing how comfortable he is, eating pizza on my couch, in my house, in my space. I am internally screaming. I don't allow men into my house for a reason—I have no control. There is no way Jace and I would ever happen but I have this sick issue where anytime I get stressed with school or work, I end up under a man, in bed, having sex. Which I tend to regret because it always ends up leaving me unsatisfied. I mean, c'mon, how hard is it to find the clit? Do I need to put a diamond on it? Need a tattoo saying, *lick here*? Write down a fantasy football draft sheet ending at the clit?

"What are we watching?" Jace asks as he leans down to grab a second slice.

I give in, grabbing the second box under the disgusting pineapple and ham and opening it to see a normal cheese pizza. "*True Blood*."

"What is it about?"

"Vampires," I say.

"Like that one guy who sparkles and the girl whose facial expression makes her look constipated?"

I turn to him, shaking my head. "What? No. That's *Twilight*. This"—I point to the TV— "is the adult version."

"Well, this main character is annoying already. Like she has a stick up her ass," he says as he stares at the TV.

I tuck my legs under me, turning toward him and pointing my pizza slice in his face. "Do not ever disrespect Anna Paquin like that again. She is a classic and deserves a lot more credit. She's from New Zealand. Aren't you guys supposed to stick up for each other or something?" I turn my body away from him, taking a bite of pizza to hide my smile because I know he is not from New Zealand. I just wanted to piss him off.

He drops his arm from the top of the couch, and I can feel his eyes burn a hole in the side of my face. "I am from Ireland."

"To-may-to, to-mah-to," I say, waving my hand in the air to brush the fact off.

"What? What is that supposed to mean? Aren't ye in college? Do you not know your countries?"

"Do you not know when you're an uninvited guest?" I turn to look at him, sucking the pizza crust dust off my fingers. He stares at me with a blank face, completely oblivious. "When are you leaving?"

"Look…" He digs his fingers into his eyes. "I don't want to be here—"

"Oh great! Something we can agree on." I force my attention back to the TV. I am missing out on one of my favorite episodes because of him. My comfort show may be a little outrageous but—Actually, there is no "but." It's outrageous. I've watched every season more than twice and I love it. End of story.

"I am not leaving until Rowan and Celeste come back," Jace finishes.

"And when will they be back?" I ask. How am I supposed to walk around the house naked and sing terribly at the top of my lungs when I'm having a bad day? Or get so drunk from wine that I fall asleep barely hanging onto the couch?

"A while," he says.

He doesn't want to be here as much as I don't want him here, but he is forced to be here on Rowan's order. Maybe if I make his life absolute hell, he will take off and tell Rowan he couldn't do it.

I fake-sigh, stretching my arms out above my head and lying down on the couch. I extend my legs out and push all my force into Jace's leg.

"Can ye not?"

I peek my head above my shoulder to look at him. "Can *you* not?"

His eyebrows furrow. "I am not doing anything."

"Uh, yes. You're in my vicinity!"

He makes a weird scoffing noise before scooting over to give me more room. I lie my head back down in my hands with a grin on my face. I am going to make sure this babysitting gig is a job from hell for him, but before I can think of the next destructive and annoying thing to do, I hear my phone ring and turn the TV volume down to walk to my bedroom and answer it. When I pick it up, I see the caller ID is unknown.

"Hello?"

"Hey, Lily."

I stand in silence before the voice finally clicks.

Oh my god. I run back to my bedroom door, slamming it shut. "Where the fuck are you? This fucking Irish lover boy is refusing to leave our house. He said something about you and Rowan having an emergency? Made me pack clothes for you and told me you would be gone for a while. What the fuck is going on?! Jesus, Celeste, when I said go talk to the man, I didn't mean disappear with him as well!"

Celeste responds by telling me she is fine, and they are in Italy. She doesn't know how long they are going to be there and Jace is here to watch me, and she tells me to be *nice*. I explain to her in very vivid detail how I am not going to be *nice* and that I told him to leave, I don't need a babysitter, and that she knows how I get when I am stressed and around men!

When I finally stop babbling, I realize the other side of the line is too quiet. "Oh my god, Celeste! Are you listening to me?!"

"Yes, I am here."

I roll my eyes. She was not listening. When she gets home, I am going to strangle her to death.

"Look, I will call you as much as I can. Just don't do anything stupid," she pleads.

"Anything stupid? Are you kidding me right now?"

The line starts beeping.

Wow. She hung up on me. I throw my phone on the bed, walking back out to the living room and sitting on the couch. Jace is completely in his own world, working on his laptop again.

I clear my throat. "So, just got off the phone with Celeste. She told me that you don't need to be here. So, you can leave now."

"If you want some privacy to watch your porn, I can go into another room." He turns to me with a smirk on his face.

I look toward the TV to see the very vivid sex scene on the screen. My cheeks burn up as if I'm standing ten feet away from the sun. I continue to avoid his eye contact and say, "It's not porn. It's quality entertainment."

"Yeah, porn-o-holics say the same thing."

I think I hate him.

I hate him.

I hate him.

Chapter Three

Jace

♫ "Duality" - Slipknot ♫

This is wrong. Oh-so very feckin' wrong. I tap on her shoulder, trying to wake up Lily, who is currently stroking my cock. I don't remember when we fell asleep on the couch, or when her head fell into my lap with her hand grabbing my dick.

This is so wrong, but fuck, it feels good. I tap on her shoulder harder when my dick starts twitching. Her hand squeezes my tip, and my head falls back on the couch. I lift my head up and shove at her shoulder. I can see the side of her face as her eyes pop open and her fingers spread out, hovering inches above my crotch.

I think she just processed what she was doing.

She jumps off the couch with her legs tangled in the blanket, causing her to fall back and land on her arse. "What are you doing?!" she yells.

"What am I doing?" I reach for a throw pillow, putting pressure on my dick. "*Álainn,* what are you doing? Why were you grabbing my dick?"

"I-I was not! Why was your dick in my hand?!"

Fuck. I run my hands through my hair. My eyes follow Lily as she runs out of the living room to her bedroom, slamming her door shut without another word. I rest my head back against the couch and close my eyes. I have had a slight boner since the moment Lily opened the door, showing the whole neighborhood her feckin' silky legs. Now that ghost feeling of her hand wrapped around my cock will never go away.

I thrust my head up when her bedroom door re-opens and she runs, disappearing into the opposite hallway, returning only a few seconds later with a pile of clothes in her hands. She runs back to her bedroom, slams her door shut again, but leaves a trail of clothes behind her.

A gruffly moan leaves my mouth as I throw the pillow off me, standing and readjusting my dick. I gather all her clothes from the floor and knock on her door.

"Not now, Jace!"

I knock again, my third knock cut off as Lily swings the door open with her jeans barely on her hips, unbuttoned, showing off her panties.

Feckin' shit.

"What?!" she yells.

I hold out her clothes. She stares at her panties that are wrapped between my fingers, her cheeks turning bright strawberry pink. She looks up at me, snatches them out of my hands, and tries to shut the door on me, but I keep it open with my foot and lean against the frame. "I'm taking you to work."

She gets on the floor on all fours, looking under her bed. "No, you're not," she says, getting up while holding one shoe and running to her en-suite.

I follow her into her room and stand in the entry to her bathroom. She finds the other shoe under a towel on the floor. I watch as she tries to balance on one leg to put them on.

"My orders were to stay with you. So yes, I am taking you to work."

"I can take the subway," she quickly responds without looking at me. She rotates to the mirror, throwing her hair into a high ponytail.

"You're late, no, *álainn?* You won't make it to the subway."

She drops her shoulders, and her big emerald eyes meet mine. "Fine, this one time. But only because I am late!"

We get into my car and before I start the engine, I turn to look at her, waiting.

"What?! C'mon! You're going to make me late!"

"Seatbelt," I demand.

She rolls her eyes, buckling herself in. I start my car and my music starts playing loudly through the speakers.

"Ugh! What is wrong with you people?" her arms cross over her chest as she shakes her head.

"What?"

"How can you listen to this screaming music all day?"

I lift one eyebrow, turning to look at her. "You work at the club that plays this screaming music all day."

"I hide my headphones under my hair." She gives me a wide smile that protrudes her dimples high on her cheeks before she turns to face the window.

I turn the music up louder and step on the gas when I pull out into the street. I can see her body tense in the corner of my eye when I hit ninety miles an hour. I curl my hand tighter around the steering wheel, fighting back a smile. Not many people can drive through traffic in New York like I can. I've been driving here since I was thirteen. So, memorizing the streets, when and where traffic is going to be the worst, and how to lane change without sideswiping someone is a fucking talent for me.

Less than ten minutes later, we pull into Caffee Latte. Lily turns to me before getting out and says, "Remind me to never get in a car with you again."

I don't respond to her, because she *will* get in the car with me again. She wanted to get to work on time, so I got her to work on time. I follow her into the coffee shop and grab a table in the far corner where nobody can sit behind me. I watch as she replaces the cashier up front, plasters a smile on her face, and starts taking orders. She has one of those smiles that can make anyone's day better. She could walk into a room, and everyone would stop to look at her like she radiates sunshine. She has been my obsession since the day I met her at Club Opal. An obsession I have not been able to overcome.

I saw her plump lips, crystal green eyes, ivory skin, and I instantly developed this desire, hunger, craving—a need to be with her, learn her, watch her every move. Her snarky, pretentious attitude only makes me want her more. I know everything about her, yet she wants nothing to do with me.

Luckily for her, I am a patient man. A smart predator is a patient one and I have the mental capacity to endure a challenge. I like to sit. Wait. Wait for my meal to let their guard down before I feast.

Unfortunately, my predator instinct was killed as soon as I got the phone call from Rowan. Now here I am, sitting like feckin' prey in this shitty coffee shop, watching her work. I stop staring at her and open the DWYM program. Do What You Must is a private investigation company that Rowan and I created. We only take certain customers, and we do questionable things to get the job done.

My eyes roam back to where Lily stands, unable to keep my eyes off her. The line to order is long and next in line is a man wearing a suit I know he can't afford. I watch Lily's face contort. Her eyes go low like a little siren in the ocean calling for a sailor. She props her elbows on the counter, putting her head in her hands. Her elbows press against her breasts, pushing them outward.

On command, my legs staring moving, making my way to the front counter. I stand by this lad, towering over him by almost two feet. As I stare down at him, he tries to puff his chest out at me. I don't retreat, I don't flinch. I just let the heat flow down my skin into my clenched fist. After a while, he gets nervous, breaking eye contact, and steps aside.

I turn my head to see Lily standing away from the counter, her nose and eyebrows scrunched. "What the fuck, Jace?"

"Black coffee, no sugar."

"No. You cannot cut in line."

A man steps behind Lily, wiping his hand on a cloth before running his fingers through his salt and pepper hair. He is barely her height, but he keeps his head held high as if he has his own podium to stand on.

"What is going on here?"

"Black coffee. No sugar." I push a hundred-dollar bill on the counter, toward whom I am assuming is Lily's boss. "Keep the change."

He stares at the bill as if he has never seen green paper before. He rips it off the counter, holding it up to the light and looking back at me, then gives me a broken smile. He slowly turns to Lily and screams, "You heard the man, Lilith! Get the coffee!"

I shove my clenched fist into my jean pockets. Lily looks at me, rolling her eyes, and turns around to pour coffee into a cup. She turns back and slides it on the counter, but purposely tips the cup over, making the steaming coffee spill over the bar and onto my jeans.

"Whoopsie," she says, raising her chin in the air with gleaming eyes.

"Fuck, Lilith." Her boss rounds the counter with a white towel and starts to wipe off any coffee that dripped onto my jeans and shoes. He gets on one knee, rubbing the towel at my jeans and way too close to my crotch for comfort.

"I am sorry about that, sir. She is a nitwit. I swear, I don't know why I hired her."

I break my eye contact with Lily, looking down at the man at my feet. I grab him by the collar of his shirt, pulling him up into the air until his toes barely touch the ground. I can hear people in line behind me gasp and whisper. Her boss's eyes look like they are going to pop out of their sockets and his mouth hangs open.

"Apologize." The lad starts to tremble in my grasp, pulling at my arm to try and make me let him go. "Apologize," I grit again between my teeth.

"I'm sorry!" he cries.

My blood boils, ready to put her boss six feet in the ground for disrespecting a woman, *my woman*. If she is Lilith, then I am the king of hell, and he better pray to a god for salvation because deliverance doesn't come from my hands.

I pull him closer to my face. "I think you can do a bit better than that, can't ye?"

"I'm so sorry Lily—" I tighten my hold on his shirt, hearing his cheap cotton rip beneath my fingers. "You're a fantastic employee. I didn't mean it."

I use my other hand to reach into his front left pocket, right where my hundred-dollar bill was pocketed by this greedy, narcissistic fuck. I bet he doesn't pay his employees enough, probably evades taxes. It would be really unfortunate if his business came crumbling down one day. I slide the money over to Lily. "Pay for my coffee, *álainn*, and the rest is yours."

I wait for her to finish grabbing her tip from the cash register before I set her boss down. I brush my hand against his shirt collar, trying to fix the wrinkles and rips. "What's your name, lad?"

"Mart."

"Mart, what?"

"Mart Carmichael."

I hum and pat him on top of his head. "That wasn't so hard, was it, Mart?"

He shakes his head, trying to stop the bitch tears from falling down his face. I lean in and whisper to him. When I straighten back, he slowly starts to back away, turning on his heel to run to the back of the shop.

I turn to Lily, who is staring at me. Another employee is whispering in her ear behind her, but smiling at me, clearly infatuated with what just happened.

I walk back to my table, sitting, as everyone continues to steal little glances at me. I notice one person on the phone, probably some feckin' *bollock* calling the cops.

Lily comes to stand in front of me, removing her apron. "What did you say to him?"

"Did he just fire you? Because if he did, then—"

She holds out her hand to stop me. "I'm quitting before he has the chance to fire me."

I shake my head, sitting back down. "You don't have to quit if you don't want to. He won't fire you."

She sits down in the seat across from me. "What did you say to him?" she whispers.

"That if he ever makes any derogatory remarks about you again that I will remove the skin off his bones and mail it to his family." I shrug.

She bites at her cheeks, looking around at everything but me. "How do you know where his family is?"

I nod toward the front door, hearing sirens in the distance. "We should probably go before they show up."

We walk out of the coffee shop, straight to my vehicle. I unlock my car, opening the passenger door for her to get in, and make my way around to the driver-side door.

"You didn't have to do all that," Lily says when I enter my vehicle.

"He was an asshole who deserved it."

"Okay, but no need to go all *Superman* on him."

"I prefer Bane," I say.

She gives me a screwed-up look. "What?"

I hear the sirens getting closer from down the street and quickly make a sharp turn down an alley to head the back way toward her house. "You know, Bane, from *Batman*."

She rolls her eyes. "Whatever. Just drop me off at home and go back to *Gotham*, Bane. I can handle myself."

I take my eyes off the road, turning to her. Her emerald eyes have hints of hazel that break through in the sunlight. She took her hair out of her ponytail so it lies just past her shoulders, waving around like in the Van Gogh painting. Her button nose and pink puckered lips are perfectly disproportioned on her face. Her nose is too small, her lips and eyes too big. Yet they are all perfectly imperfect on her. "Yeah, I'm sure you can," I respond.

As soon as I pull up to her house, she jumps out of the car before I am fully in park. I watch her run up the stairs, shutting the door behind her. When I go to open her front door, it doesn't budge. I shake my head, laughing, taking two steps back before I run full speed, and crash my shoulder into the cheap wood. It cracks slightly and I hear the chains and bolts fall to the floor on the opposite side. I slam my fist into the crack, breaking open a hole right near the doorknob. I unlock the door, ramming it open forcefully so it crashes against her wall.

I stand in the doorway, staring at her, watching her fingers wiggle at her side.

"This is breaking and entering. I am calling the cops." She darts toward her bedroom, slamming that door shut.

I close the broken door behind me and stalk toward her bedroom door. It could be locked, it could be unlocked, it doesn't matter. I still shove my shoulder into the door, breaking it to where it barely hangs from the hinges. She stands near her bed with her phone in her hand and her face a ghostly white. I stride to her, rip the phone away from her, and toss it onto the bed. I wrap one arm around her hips, picking her up off the ground, and walk toward her desk, using my free hand to wipe away all her clutter and sitting her down with my hands plastered at her hips to keep her trapped in front of me.

"No need to get the authorities involved now, yeah?"

She turns her face away from mine, her cheeks turning crimson as she bites down on her bottom lip. I grab her by her chin, making her face me again. I catch her slight glance at my lips, and it makes her pupils dilate big enough to invade her irises.

"As soon as Rowan and Celeste are back, I will leave you and your porn alone," I say, bringing up her TV show from last night. "But until then…" Her eyes close and I can hear her deep inhale. I take the chance and turn her head to the side to get closer to the little part of her neck right between her shoulder, sucking in her sweet smell. "I will be at your side, watching your every move like a fucking Peregrine," I whisper against her skin.

I drop the hold I have on her chin, backing away. Her eyes slowly open as she breathlessly says, "The term is hawk. Watching your every move like a hawk."

"I like Peregrine Falcon better." I turn around, walking out of her room, leaving the mess of wooden door chips and paperwork all over the floor.

"You're going to pay for new doors and locks!" she screams.

I sit at the kitchen table, finishing all the events in the DWYM program from the other night. I add in all the events of Rowan's house, from the killings to the cleaning, and add in me going to John's house. I never liked John. He always pissed me off with his big body and bald head—and now that he has disappeared after the break in and is not answering anyone's calls, it makes me hate him even more.

I turn my head when I hear a door scraping along the floor. Lily is trying to push her bedroom door open. I prop my elbow on the table and watch her struggle.

"I have to go to work. You coming, falcon?"

"Are you going to behave yourself and not run off?" I stand from my chair, walking toward her. I can see her pupils enlarge again. Either she did plan on running off, or she's intimidated, and it turns her on. I move a strand of hair out of her face, tucking it behind her ear. "Don't test my patience, *álainn.*"

"That's not English, is it?"

"No," I say, grabbing her arm to walk her to the front door.

Rowan's house being broken into by some ex-Italian mafia members puts us on the map. And if it puts Rowan and me on the map, then anyone we are close to gets put on the map. Which includes Celeste and Lily. If anything happened to Lily, I would kill myself. Then Rowan would bring me back to life and murder me for upsetting Celeste by letting something happen to her best friend.

When we are both at my car doors, I press the unlock button, but before we get in, I look at her and remind her, "Do not run."

Chapter Four

Lily

♫ "Howlin' for you" - The Black Keys ♫

My stomach churns as Jace races through the streets of New York. This is the most traumatizing afternoon I have ever experienced. Jace drives as if there is no one on the road beside him. Not only am I getting car-sick, but I am also starting to worry about Celeste. She called me from an unknown number, which means she probably doesn't have her phone. And Jace is holding me hostage as if the Boogieman were out to get us. I take a deep breath, closing my eyes.

I will not throw up in this man's car.

I will not throw up in this man's car.

I will not throw up in this man's car.

I pinch my eyes tighter since I'm sure I just heard a lady scream as we drove by. I would not doubt that he almost ran someone over. If I continue to keep my eyes closed, then I won't see anything more traumatizing—like his shoulder easily ramming through two of my doors in the house. Or the way his large arm felt around my hips as he picked me up like a rag doll and shoved all my schoolwork to the ground, then proceeded to get way too close for comfort. God, he smelled good. I had to close my eyes just to gather myself. And when he smiles, I feel my heart stop as if I have never been smiled at before. His teeth are perfectly straight, white, and his anterior teeth are insanely sharp—like vampire sharp.

No more watching True Blood for me.

I open my eyes when I no longer feel the sun beating on my skin, and look around to see we're driving through the underground parking garage of Club Opal. I turn to Jace, asking, "How do you have passage here?" You have to have a key card to enter, and you must pay the yearly fee on top of the club entry fee.

"I know Axel."

"How?" Axel, my boss, that I have never met before, tends to stay locked in his office located on the top floor. He has a large window that faces the club floor so he can watch all his little demons run around. Anytime we need something from him, we are met by his assistant, Roxxie. Roxxie hands us our checks and new contracts every year. The contract always states "no phones, no speaking of anything you hear or see in the club outside of work," blah blah blah. I don't care what the contract says. I sign the dotted line every year once I read I'm getting paid fifty dollars an hour, plus tips.

"History," Jace says.

We turn to face each other at the same time. Why is he so secretive about everything? I am an open book, but with this man, you obviously have to beat the shit out of him with a hammer just to have him pony up a secret.

Ignoring him, I roll up my knee-high stockings and pull down my deep V-neck shirt, lifting my breasts up to my neck, then switch from my slippers to my heels. When I look back at Jace, his freckles are slightly covered in a pink hue and he clenches his jaw before turning away from me.

We enter the club from the back and see Roxxie standing behind the red rope, stopping anyone from going upstairs. She guards those stairs like a Bloodhound.

"Good evening, Mr. Cook. Axel is waiting for you," Roxxie says.

Jace turns away from Roxxie, grabbing my arm, and mouths, *"Do not run."*

I roll my eyes, pulling my arm out of his grasp, and walk away. His parents must hate him if they named him Jace Cook. As I walk deeper into the club, I see Marge sitting at one of the sectionals, working on the floor chart.

"Hey baby," she says to me while grabbing my arm, pulling me down to sit next to her.

Marge is the mom of all of us at the club. She has worked here the longest and keeps all of us in check. Today she is wearing a see-through, all-black leotard that cuts deep in the back and the front, with knee-high strappy boots.

"Hi Marge." I squeeze her hand, leaning in to peek at the floor chart.

"Do you want the L or six through eight?" she asks.

"Give me the L. I need the money." I wink at her as she goes to write my name on the seating chart.

I swear I am her favorite. I don't ever see her asking any of the other tenders what sections they want. We are called tenders because we are not technically bartenders, and we are not servers. We *tend* to our customers' needs. Sometimes we bring drinks, sometimes we sit with our customers to keep them happy, and sometimes we take the customers in the back to "relax."

Secretly, of course.

Most of the men who come here are some of the richest men in New York. They have reputations, wives, kids. That is why everything that happens in this club cannot be spoken about. I have never taken anyone back, and don't ever plan to. All my regulars know this and don't even bother asking me. I've witnessed tenders take customers into the back and within weeks, the customers become jealous and overprotective. That's why I stick to the saying, "Don't shit where you eat."

"Look what the skank dragged in."

I turn my head to see Rebecca walking up to me and Marge. I pinch the bridge of my nose and say, "I knew I smelled fish."

Rebecca punches me in the arm with a smile on her face. She leans in and kisses my cheek. "How you doin'?" she asks with her Jersey accent.

"Oh, you know, just peachy."

"What is peachy is that ass of yours. You look good today." She bends down to look at the floor chart. "And you're in the L. You here to make money today, aren't you?"

I shrug my shoulders. "A girl has to pay rent somehow." I stand off the couch, pulling my shirt down more and lifting my breasts while giving Rebecca a wink. I walk away to the locker room and grab my phone from my waistband, tucking it into my locker.

Shit. Jace had me so distracted trying to be a macho man that I forgot my headphones at home. Which means I will have to listen to some snotty rich men talk about their lives over the blasting screamo music all night.

I sit down on the bench, fixing my shoes, and turn my head to see the other tenders in the corner near a table. They pass around a rolled-up dollar bill, snorting. This job isn't hard, but it's not easy, either. We practically act like therapists to grown men, but instead of being in a professional setting where the therapist is ten feet away from them in a suit, we are half naked, serving them alcohol while they rub their clammy fingers on our bodies. *If we allow it.* Marge and I are some of the only tenders who are off limits. Marge only allows certain people, if she likes them. And I'm a "look-y don't touch-y."

The lights start to dim, and I can feel the vibrations through the floor in my feet.

Show time.

I pinch the bridge of my nose, trying to force the pressure out of my head. Tonight was not the night to forget headphones. I'm sitting next to a group of older men as they laugh and choke at whatever they deem funny. I have my elbow propped along the top of the couch with my head in my hand, fake laughing and smiling on cue with them.

I need a drink. I lean in, whispering to—fuck what was his name? "I'll be back with a new bottle," I say, smiling.

"Okay, Candy, don't take too long."

I stand off the couch, turning away and rolling my eyes. Candy? Where the fuck did he get that name from? I start walking toward the back of the club, passing by the VIP section. I glance around and land on Jace's open curtains. His elbows are leaning on his knees while he types on his phone. As if he could feel me staring, his eyes jump up to look at me. I use my middle finger to rub the tip of my nose.

Slowly, he leans back along the couch, throwing his arms over the top and spreading his legs open. I look away, rolling my eyes. Maybe this is why I have a headache. All the shit I've dealt with the past two days could put me in a hospital for brain damage.

I walk past all the VIP sections into the back room where we hide all the liquor. At Club Opal, there is no bar. So, we are forced to come back here and get the bottles ourselves. The collection is insane. I have never had a customer come in here and ask for a bottle we don't have.

I grab a bottle of vodka and a glass, pouring myself a double shot. It tastes so good and so bad at the same time. After choking it down, I turn to search our wall of liquor until I find the two-hundred-dollar tequila bottle. I grab it by the handle and turn to leave out the door, but almost fall on my ass when I run into a wall.

I bend my neck back, seeing Jace standing in front of me. "Jesus, Jace, what are you doing?"

His eyes travel from my head to my toes and his jaw tenses. "Come to my section."

"No. I have a section. That you can clearly see me from. Don't worry, I'm not planning on running," I snap, taking two steps back.

"I know you're not. I know I can see you."

"So, what is the problem?" I ask.

He takes two steps forward, then another, backing me into the wall. I can feel the cold bricks on my back, sending chills down my body. He plants his hands on both sides of my face, leaving no room for me to move around him. His biceps are so large they could squish me like a bug. His blonde hair shags over his forehead and fades on the side. I try not to breathe. If I breathe, I will smell him, his spicy, woody scent—and god, it smells so good.

I hold the bottle to my chest, trying to separate him for me, trying to leave room for Jesus. My breathing starts to become erratic, and I feel extremely vulnerable back here as he continues to stare at me, not saying anything. I watch his blue eyes move from mine, down to my lips, down to my chest. I swear, if he kisses me, I will slap him.

"Mr. Cook, Axel would like to see you again."

I bend to look under Jace's arm to see Roxxie standing behind us with her hands behind her back. Her hair is always in a perfect short pixie cut. She has strong, defined features and beautiful, tan glowing skin. Yet she acts like a robot. No emotion. It's quite terrifying, yet attractive, and I would so kiss her right now for saving me.

I stand up straight, still pinned under Jace. "They're calling you, *dog*," I say with a smirk. He is always being told what to do and where to go. "*Jace come here, Jace go there*." Someone get this man a collar and a leash.

His lip twitches in response and a grunt comes from his throat, making my heart stop and my face fall. He pushes himself off the wall, puts his hands in his front pockets, and turns to follow Roxxie out of the room.

I lean my head against the wall and press my body further against it, needing it to swallow me whole.

Chapter Five

Lily

♫ "Bad Intentions (feat. Migos)" - Niykee Heaton ♫

I finally get cut at 1 a.m. I say goodbye to my drunk, remaining customers and head for the locker room. I grab my cell phone and sit on the bench to roll down my itchy stockings while pulling out the cash from my bra to count.

Fifteen hundred dollars.

Mateo, one of my regulars who comes in, tips me five hundred dollars every time he is here. I know it's only because he wants to take me out to dinner—which I refuse every time. I just sit there and talk to him. He's only a couple of years older than me, not bad looking. Typical dark brown hair, brown eyes, an insanely pointy cupid's bow, no piercings, no tattoos, just a typical New York businessman—a rich New York businessman.

I spot Jace leaning on the wall with his arms crossed against his chest when I walk out of the locker room. "Can we stop somewhere? I'm hungry," I propose, pushing all my money back into my bra.

He propels himself off the wall and starts walking away.

"Is that a yes?" I follow him out the back door of the club. The cool breeze hits my uncovered legs and arms, making my teeth chatter. I wrap my arms along my body and start jogging toward the car. I beat Jace there, pulling on the handle. When I look up, I can see him striding, taking his time.

"Please open it," I beg.

He puts his hand in his pocket and starts walking slower.

I let go of the car door handle, putting my hands on my hips. "I will break your window."

"And I will break you," he states.

That literally makes no sense. As I am about to give him my middle finger, the car automatically turns on. I pull on the handle, quickly get inside, and reach for a knob to turn the heater on. I pause, my hand mid-air as I look at all the electronics. What kind of technology is this? There are multiple buttons at the bottom, mainly the push start and a huge knob at the top. None of them look remotely close to being a heater or AC. Why have a half a million-dollar car if you have to struggle just to find the heat or AC buttons?

Jace opens the driver-side door, throwing me a sweater. "Where do you want to get food?"

Oh god, it smells like him and it's so soft. I run my hands over it. It has to be a hundred percent wool. I look at the tag to read the very famous, very popular, very expensive name brand. I slam my eyes shut, scared to look anymore. I would die to have at least one thing from their collections. I bring the sweater closer to my face, looking at the knitting. This must be their Pont Neuf yarn.

"Lily?"

I snap my head to look at him.

"Do I need to leave you so you can continue eye fucking my sweater or do you want to go somewhere to eat?" he teases.

I can feel the warmth in my cheeks. My fingers clench the sweater. "Food. Yes." I place the sweater neatly into my lap because for one, if I put it on, I will never take it off. Two, because it smells like him and there is a chance I won't take it off for that reason as well. Three, I just won't take it off.

"Can we go to Hippies?" I ask.

"Hippies?"

"Yes, have you never been there?" I pull my legs under me, my eyes growing bigger as I turn to him. My mouth waters just thinking about it. "They make the best sandwiches."

"Hippies it is."

What I may have failed to mention to Jace is that it is an hour away, and at this time of night, the line is extremely long.

After a thirty-minute wait, we finally pull up to the speaker.

"What do you want?"

I bend closer to Jace, looking out the window. My eyes light up as I stare at the menu. "A double-double, large fries, and a fruity Judy," I state.

"What the fuck is a fruity Judy?" He turns his head and our lips slightly brush from how far I'm leaning over. I fall back into my seat as we gawk at each other.

The intercom asked what we wanted, but we're stuck staring at each other. The muscle in his jaw constricts and my heart hammers in my chest. I clench the sweater in my lap, forcing my fingers to not touch the tingly sensation I received from his lips touching mine. I have never had that happen before. Why did that happen? Why do I want to lean over and experience it again? Maybe I will. Should I? I mean, why not? He is handsome, like really handsome. I can admit that. I just hate him, maybe we can hate fuck. I heard those always end well. Maybe he knows how to put that lean, toned body of his to use. I might just let him. I can get it out of my system, we can do it for one night, and then go back to hating each other.

Finally, he breaks off our eye contact and orders my food. I watch as his fingers tightly grip the steering wheel, driving to the first window. His arm is covered in tattoos from his fingertips up to the side of his neck, crossing to his other arm. I notice something that looks like wings, another that looks like a scythe, and the rest I can't see in the dark.

"It's their signature drink. A bunch of fruit juices mixed together. Goes good with vodka," I say, my fingers rubbing the fabric of the sweater.

"And is that what you're doing tonight? Getting drunk?"

I shrug my shoulders. "I mean, I no longer have a morning job, thanks to you." That gets his attention. His eyes bounce to me, blazing. I clear my throat. "I can't decide if it's a good or bad thing for me yet. I rarely make it to class, even though most of my classes are online. I mean, we don't have to drink if you don't want to. I mean, I don't even know if I want to. It's like two a.m. Who starts drinking this late at night, or early in the morning? However you take it. Did you know that vodka used to be used as an antibacterial agent?"

His eyebrows pinch forward as he studies me, but I can't stop the word-vomit that is coming out of my mouth. "From the way it tastes, it makes sense. Pour a little on a cut and it will be disinfected. And vodka is a diminutive of *voda*, which means water in Russian. Vodka is really big in Russia, right? Do you know? You probably don't know. You're from Ireland, so why would you know? Yet I'm from Greece and I know, but I don't know why I know. I just like learning random little facts about things I guess." I finally exhale, shutting my mouth and turning to look out the passenger window.

Jesus Christ, Lily, pull it together.

The window opens. "That will be three seventy-five."

I go to reach into my purse on the floor, but a large hand stops me, grabbing my wrist. When I look up, Jace is exchanging his card for the greasy, delicious bag.

He hands me the bag and says, "I am nervous that you're about to eat a fried bologna *piece* that only cost a dollar."

"Piece? It's called a sandwich. A double stacked sandwich," I correct. "If you're nice, I will let you have a bite." I give him a hospitable smile, but I see his fingers turn white on the steering wheel.

If I don't get out of this car right now, I might end up having a nervous breakdown. I have never had a nervous breakdown around men. That slight kiss? Lip brush? Peck? Whatever it was made me fucking nervous. It felt too… real? Too nice? And according to the way he is gripping the steering wheel for his dear life—it seems as if he is nervous too.

I'm not stupid. I know Jace finds me attractive. Ever since I dropped off a bottle for Jace and Rowan in their section years ago, he has always had his eyes on me. Always trying to talk to me while I'm working, or constantly staring at me, creeping me out. I am afraid the longer I am with him, the more nervous I will get. I will end up saying something even stupider. I wonder if we have a quick hate fuck, will my brain calm down? Will I no longer be nervous and get over whatever feeling this is? Will I still be worried about being down one job, or the current assignment I have due that I haven't started, or the fact that Celeste and I haven't paid the utility bill yet and I have no idea when we will since she is MIA? Okay, I need to calm down. Now. Don't think about anything stressful. Or Jace. Or sex. Fuck, I should probably see a therapist.

For me, sex is just fucking. I don't understand the need to have to love someone to have sex with them. Sex is a temporary energy exchange. A physical serotonin exchange from one person to the other. I don't need to know where your mother grew up, how many siblings you have, or what your five-year life goal plan is. As long as you're not my regular customer at work, I am down. Which Jace is not, because he stays in VIP, where I do not tend to.

I can differentiate between making love and fucking, and I'd rather take the latter. We can hate-fuck, get it out of our system, and worry about the possible awkward interactions after Rowan and Celeste come home. He is totally my type: blonde hair and blue eyes. He's covered in tattoos, muscular, annoying, possessive, and controlling. It's all the red flags a girl can dream of—for one night.

Chapter Six

Jace

♫ "Human" – Sevdaliza ♫

Lily stops at the front door when she notices she has a new door and locks. I called in a lad to come fix both her doors. Her front door has a new keypad lock that includes fingerprints, along with an inside security blocker. The only fingerprints in the system are hers and Celeste's.

And Rowan's... and mine.

I step around her to enter the code on the keypad.

"Yeah, you need to teach me how to change the code."

I nod, opening the door for her. She walks into the kitchen, looking over her shoulder at me with a seductive smile. She puts her food on the kitchen counter and walks to her bedroom door, shutting it.

I sit at the kitchen island and pull my laptop out to start working on the two cases Axel referred to Rowan and me. One is for some shit-head named Mateo Davenport.

Recently he tried to divorce his wife, who mysteriously disappeared with his money and a family heirloom. He hasn't heard from the wife in over three months. Surprisingly, he doesn't want his money back. He is more focused on us finding her, getting back the family heirloom, and keeping it out of the media.

I pull up our program to do a search on Mateo. He is a broker, works on Wall Street at the top of his company. He has a net worth of $2.3 billion with three divorces under his belt already—four if you count Ms. Ava, the mystery woman who disappeared.

There is a good reason he has been divorced multiple times in the past two years, and I don't think getting the family heirloom is his priority. We do this for a living, and sometimes our clients think we are stupid. We have seen everything. Any and all types of scenarios.

I hear Lily's door open, then see her step out of her room dressed in a tight V-neck T-shirt with little shorts and knee-high socks. It leaves absolutely nothing to the imagination. I try to swallow but my throat feels constricted as my eyes follow her footsteps to the kitchen. She picks up her food and makes her way to the living room to sit her pretty little arse down on the couch.

"Take a break, let's watch something together," she says with a smile, showing off those two dimples.

No muscles in my body move as I stare at her. I watch her hand pat the couch right next to her, suggesting where to sit. I look at my computer, slowly blinking. I have not entered anything in the program and it's already 3 a.m. I turn back to Lily, seeing her eat her fries while she channels surfs the TV. One episode won't hurt. Once she falls asleep, I will continue entering my notes in the program.

I walk to the couch, sitting feet away from her.

"What do you want to watch?" she asks.

"Anything except your porn."

She rolls her eyes and puts on the porn show. I pretend not to watch her open the greasy bag and pull out the *piece*— or sandwich, as she corrected me. She swiftly unwraps the sandwich and takes a bite. Her head falls back, a moan leaving her mouth. My hands stiffen on the couch at the silky, seductive sound. Fuck Rowan for putting me through this torture. The motherfucker did this on purpose, I know he did. I have to keep reminding myself I am here for her protection. To make sure nothing happens to her. But if she makes that noise again, there is nothing on this earth that would protect her from me.

I think about her at the club tonight, entertaining all those men while they looked at her like she was some slab of meat. I wanted her in the VIP room with me so that I wouldn't get kicked out for splitting someone's jaw in half—especially Mateo's. He keeps Lily entertained. They talked for most of the night. He ignored all his colleagues and just faced Lily, kept her fucking smiling.

Feckin' smiling.

Lily squirms on the couch as she uses her thumb to wipe off whatever sauce is on the corner of her mouth, then sucks on her thumb, cleaning it off.

"Want a bite?"

I look between her and the sandwich. She gets on her knees, crawling to me on the couch, holding out the sandwich in one hand.

"It tastes so good," she whispers.

My fingers grasp the couch as I feel my cock spring against my zipper. She's only inches away from me, her chest pressing against the side of my arm. With one rapid move, she throws her leg over me, straddling my waist.

"*Álainn,* what are you doing?" I clench my teeth so hard they could crack.

"Giving you a bite," she says, smiling at me, using that seductive siren mouth of hers. I'd be damned if anyone could say no to this woman. How can I say no to this woman? She is the siren of the sea, the witch of the forest, and my fucking kryptonite.

Her hips move slightly, adjusting herself on top of me, right on my dick. I grab her waist, squeezing tightly, and close my eyes. "Don't you fucking move."

She leans closer to me, her chest pressed against mine. "Don't you want a bite, Mr. Cook?" she hums.

I crush her hips with my fingers, knowing I could possibly be leaving fingerprints. My breathing becoming erratic, feeling her hard nipples pressed against my chest with only a layer of fabric separating us. My eyes break open when I feel her breath on my lips. Her eyes meet mine for only a second before she closes hers and presses her lips softly against mine. An electric surge shocks me when our mouths connect. I move my hands from her hips, crawling up her back until I reach her neck. My finger rubs against the pulse, feeling it beat harder as I pull her deeper into me.

I squeeze her nape and she opens her mouth, letting my tongue dance against her. I break us apart and move down, leaving hungry kisses from her cheeks down to her chest. She starts to grind against my cock while running her hands through my hair. I grab her tight little shirt and rip it down the middle. A gasp leaves her mouth when I hold her breast in my hand and roam my tongue along her nipple before I close my teeth on it and pull. A moan rolls off her tongue, her head falling back as she grips the base of my hair, pulling even harder.

I could listen to that all night. I want to bask in that sound, fucking imprint it into my memory and replay it over and over again. I have waited three fucking years, three fucking long, hard years for this day.

I look up at her while sucking the next breast. She looks down at me with slightly parted lips, panting. "This is a one-time thing, Mr. Cook. I still fucking hate you."

My mouth lingers on her nipple as I stare at her, her hand reaching down to the zipper of my pants, and I grab her wrist, holding her still. Her eyes widen when she realizes I've stopped her.

She hates me. She fucking hates me. And she keeps calling me "Cook." I'm not going to fuck her if she hates me, but I will make sure she hates that we didn't fuck. I will make her loathe that we didn't fuck. I'll keep her coming and coming, until she can't fucking take it anymore, until she is begging. I will tear, rip, fucking *snatch* the hate right out of her from her fucking core.

I pick her up by her underarms and throw her body off me, her back bouncing on the couch. I finish ripping her shirt all the way off and draw a gasp from her as I lick my way down her chest to her stomach, hitting all the sensitive parts of her skin. I continue kissing, leaving marks along her skin while taking off her shorts, throwing them behind me. Grabbing her thighs, I toss them on my shoulders. Her clit glistens in the small light from the living room, our breathing the only noise surrounding us.

I use one finger to slowly graze between her lips. She is dripping. Dripping for me. She says she hates me, but her cunt says otherwise. Her eyes close and her back rises off the couch. I have one leg on the floor, holding me balanced, and my other leg bent at the knee on the couch. I drag her thighs closer to my face, leaving only her shoulders and head to touch the couch. My finger still brushes against her clit, down to her entrance.

"Please," she whispers.

I smirk at her, before bringing her sweet pussy to my lips. I widen my tongue, swiping from her entrance to flicking her clit slowly, taking my time. Worshiping this fucking siren like she deserves. I don't use too much pressure, my tongue barely skimming against her clit just enough to tease her. Yet I eat her like she is my last meal. The most delicate, expensive fucking meal I have ever had. I take my time, letting her taste invade my taste buds. Letting her scent overwhelm my smell.

Fuck, she is so divine.

"Please!" she cries.

"Please what, baby?" I stick one finger in her, curving it to hit the spot, and a scream erupts throughout the house. I can feel her clench around my two fingers, a river running between my hand and my mouth while I finger-fuck her little pussy.

I could do this for the rest of my life.

"Speak it, *álainn*. Would you like to come?" I remove myself from her.

"No!" She reaches out. "Please don't stop."

I tighten my arm that is wrapped around her waist to keep her from running away and jab three fingers inside of her, my mouth returning to her clit to play. She moans my name, her core tensing around my fingers, her thighs squeezing my face. Her hands grab onto a throw pillow above her head as I feel her body shake. I continue holding her while her body ceases, using my tongue to lick up the juices left over for me, from her center to the side of her thighs.

Such a mess we made.

When her body feels limp, I slowly drop her back onto the couch, kissing her thighs and making my way back up to her mouth. Until I hear my phone ring in the kitchen.

Feckin' bollocks.

I stand, walking to the kitchen counter. I look down at my feet when I notice I almost stepped on the sandwich Lily threw at some point. I see the caller ID, bringing my phone to my ear.

"His place was empty?"

Rowan really feels the need to call me *now* about John? I already put those events in the program earlier but for some reason, when I add events into the program, he always feels like it is a necessity to call and confirm facts.

I can feel Lily's hands on my back as she rubs around me, moving to finish unzipping my jeans.

"Empty," I reply to Rowan while trying to keep my composure. Her fingers send an electrifying current through my body.

"Have you tried to call him?"

Oh, for fuck's sake.

"Yes," I reply.

Lily finishes unzipping my jeans. I turn around to see a huge smile on her face, her dimples protruding as she bends down onto her knees in front of me. Her shirt is ripped open like a vest, her perky breasts bouncing at her movements, her shorts on the floor by her feet. The only thing left are her sexy baseball-themed knee-high socks. I keep the grin on my face when she pulls my pants slightly down and tugs my dick out of my boxers. Her eyes widen, and she bites on her bottom lip when she grabs my dick to inspect my Jacob's ladder.

"And?" Rowan asks, still on the line.

I never gave Lily a chance to taste how sweet she was in my mouth. My tongue darts out to my bottom lip, still tasting her on me. I put my phone to my chest, grab her chin with my other hand, and press hard enough for her mouth to open in shock as I spit inside her. I can see her eyes go dark as she swallows.

I put my phone to my ear again. "He didn't answer."

"Was it me or you who hired John?" Rowan asks.

So many feckin' questions right now. I set the phone down on the kitchen counter, putting it on speaker and muting it simultaneously. Lily uses her tongue to lick the pre-cum dripping from my cock. With no hesitation, she wraps her pouty lips around my head. I throw my head back, clenching my hands behind me on the counter, gripping as tight as I can. Her mouth feels so warm as she hollows out her cheeks.

I unmute the phone. "Neither of us. Your father hired him after the Club Opal incident and he just kind of never left," I tell Rowan and quickly mute the phone again. I grab Lily's hair, pushing myself deeper in her throat. "Fuck, you're such a good girl, taking all of me."

She looks up from her wet lashes, gagging and trying to push back away from me. I use my thumb to wipe the fallen tears on her cheeks and bring it to my lips to taste the saltiness of her. I want to indulge in every little thing that comes from this woman. I want her to be my demise, and I would thank her for it without remorse.

I grip the nape of her neck harder, keeping my cock deep in the back of her throat. "Breathe through your nose, *álainn.* You can take it."

"Find history on John and let me know. And Jace?" Rowan says.

I unmute the phone and clench my teeth. "What?"

"Be careful with Lily."

She smiles with my cock still deep in her mouth. She looks fucking beautiful on her knees in front of me, and I think my little siren likes the idea of sneaking around when someone can hear. I hang up the phone and smile down at her.

She pops my cock out of her mouth, giving me her seductive eyes. "Yeah, be careful with me, Jace."

"I said I would break you, didn't I?" I grip her hair and shove myself back into her.

Chapter Seven

Lily

♫ "Awkward" - SZA ♫

My heart stops when he confirms he won't be careful with me. I want that. I am tired of being handled with care and being treated like I may break into a million pieces. I need someone to find what makes my body tick, what makes me shatter like glass. I want to feel like an atomic bomb.

I shove his dick back in my mouth and use my tongue to glide along his piercings. His hands grip my hair, pulling straight from the scalp. The pain sends shards through my body, straight to my center. I open my throat, breathing though my nose like he told me to as I take him all the way to the hilt. He fills my mouth and his piercings graze along my tongue as he starts pumping.

That one hum he releases from his chest vibrates his whole body. My grip tightens on his thighs, and I pull back to twirl my tongue along the space between his shaft and head and take him back down my throat. I close my eyes and take all the pressure from him being so deep.

I want him inside me. I want to feel those piercings ripple inside me. The thought of it makes me clench my thighs together. I'm still naked from the waist down, and I can feel my juices leaking on the inside of my thighs.

His mouth opens as he pulls his dick from my mouth, stroking himself. He is about to come and I am not about to miss this. I grab his hips, pushing him back toward me, opening my mouth and closing it just at the tip, and swirl my tongue around his head. I want to taste and savor every bit of him.

"Fuck, *álainn*," he growls.

I can feel his release pile into my mouth as he puts his hands back onto the kitchen counter to catch himself. I replace his hands with mine, stroking every last drop into my mouth, swallowing everything while keeping eye contact, licking my lips.

He grabs me off the floor and I wrap my legs around him as he starts walking to the bedroom. His jeans are barely on, forcing him to wobble all the way there.

I turn to my clock to see it's 7 a.m. I'm still trying to gather myself after Jace sucked, licked, and finger-fucked me until I was coming back to back. I turn toward him to see one hand under his head, lying calm and collected, staring at the ceiling. His boxers are on, and I can still see the outline of his hard dick. We didn't have sex, but I can't complain.

I may have told him this was going to be the only time, but I want to go again. I want to have actual sex with him. He was the first man to ever give me an orgasm not once, not twice, but four times in one night. I have never experienced anything like this. I don't even know what to do now. Most men I have sex with, after they finish, they put their pants on, and say they have to dip. Or I put my clothes on and tell them I have work early in the morning—which I usually don't.

Will he go into the other room since he is technically forced to be here with me? Is he going to continue to lie here in silence until I do something? Is this the time for pillow talk? Is this the part where you ask them about their five-year life plan? What do I even say? What do I ask? *"Hey, want to put your dick in my vagina now?"*

I roll on my side toward him, opening my mouth and quickly shutting it with a small gasp. He looks at me without moving, side-eyeing me. I think I should say something.

"What are you— What are you thinking about?" I embarrassingly spit out.

Nope, this shouldn't happen. I need to get back into the streets. I am letting down the community for being this nervous around this guy.

"You," he says, turning on his side to face me. His hand brushes a piece of hair that has fallen onto my face and he softly kisses my forehead.

Oh my god. Butterflies. I have butterflies. This is a red flag, right? He is a red flag. Shit, I am the red flag! I just said I only fuck. I don't do this "make love, stay the night and cuddle" shit. Maybe I am in just in a dick trance. It will go away. It will pass.

He closes his eyes when we hear his phone ring in the other room. He huffs and retreats off the bed.

I turn to my bedside table where my phone is and send a text to Marge that I am not going to be in today. I'm also not scheduled for the whole week, which means I will be spending this whole week fucking sexy Irishman until I am over it and don't have any weird feelings toward him except for my reasonable yet unreasonable hatred toward him. I put my phone down and turn back around to see Jace standing in the doorway.

"Come here, I need to show you something."

I jump out of bed and grab the closest pair of shorts I see on the floor. I run to the living room and pause when I see the duffle bag open and filled with multiple guns. My mouth gapes as I stare at it.

I knew there were weapons in that damn bag.

He reaches down, picking up the one that lies on top, and holds it out to me. "I'm going to teach you."

"Why?" I ask.

"You need to learn. Now come here."

I take hesitant steps toward him until he pulls at my arm, putting my back against his chest. He puts the gun in my hand and points to a target that he must have taped on the wall above our kitchen. "The bullets in here aren't real. They won't kill someone, but they can do some severe damage." He sets his head right between my neck and shoulder, holding onto my hands as he shows me how to hold the gun and where the safety is. His voice trickles into my ear, causing my legs to tremble all over again. "Now point and aim in the middle," he orders.

We point the gun together and I pull the trigger. When I open my eyes—because yes, I did close them—I see I hit the target, not in the middle, but at least it was the target.

"Good. You're a natural."

Both our hands are still on the gun and I feel his finger put the safety on as he uses his head to bend my neck and start kissing me. I lean my body back into him, so ready to go again.

"Now be a good girl and go take a shower before your friend comes home, yeah?" he whispers.

"What?" I turn around as he grabs the gun from my hand and sticks it behind the couch.

"They are on their way home. You smell like sex. Go shower." He crosses his arms over his chest.

I feel my shoulders drop as I look at the ground. I called out my last day of work to be with him and now it is about to be over. This is what I wanted though, right? To fuck and get it out of my system? Well, it's not out of my system. I want more, *need* more. We didn't even fuck, he just really knows how to use that Irish mouth of his.

I pick my head back up, looking at him. "I don't smell like sex."

He stalks toward me and leans down into my face. "Oh, but you do. Now please go shower before I rip your clothes off again and take you here on these floors for our friends to see when they come home." His accent rolls off his tongue like smooth whiskey.

I stare at him, waiting, because maybe I don't want him to leave. The air in my chest constricts when he doesn't break eye contact. He slowly lifts his hand around my neck, pulling me closer to him for our lips to crash together. He wraps his tongue around mine as I dance on a cloud I never want to fall from. His hands leave my neck, picking me up by my ass. I wrap my legs around him for stability, feeling him walk toward the bedroom.

He stops kissing me and places me on my bathroom counter. He kisses my forehead and walks out of the room, closing the door behind him. I run my hands through my hair, taking a deep breath before jumping off the counter and turning on my shower.

I take a shower long enough to cool my body down. When I open my bedroom door, I can hear voices coming from outside. I quickly throw my towel on the bed, running out of the room to see the front door open, Celeste standing on the porch steps.

I sprint to her, slamming straight into her back, almost knocking us over. "Oh god, I'm so glad you are home," I say, still holding onto her. My smile falls when I see Jace getting in his car. I grab Celeste's arm, dragging her into the house.

"Did we get new doors?" she asks as she walks ahead of me into the living room.

As I am about to respond, I spot the sandwich I tossed on the floor while Jace's tongue was deep in my throat. My eyes scan the floor, trying to figure out what to do with it. My only option is to kick it under the lamp table. "Yeah, don't worry about it," I say, pushing Celeste further into the living room, toward the couch.

Thank god she didn't see that. I'll clean it up later.

Celeste tells me all about her trip while we finish a whole bottle of wine. She tells me how she went to confront Rowan about the mystery woman I took a photo of at the club. Then some big scary people came and broke into Rowan's house and Celeste hid under the table while Rowan went and killed all of them in less than ten minutes. And because Rowan was scared that they saw her car outside, they had to take off and fly to Italy in his private jet to lay low until they figured out what the hell was going on. Then she met Rowan's aunt, and she broke down that Rowan had gotten involved with the mafia.

My mind blanks out when I hear "Italian mafia." How do you accidentally get involved with the mafia? I bite on my nails, hiding my trembling lips. Jace was here to protect me. I gave him such a hard time in the beginning but all he was meant to do was protect me. Even if he was ordered to do it, I don't think he was ordered to show me how to use this fake little—but real—gun.

Clearing my throat, I say, "Don't worry, Celeste. I'll protect you."

"I love you so much, Lily, but how would you—"

I reach behind the couch, pulling out the cute little gun I now have. Celeste's eyes go wide as I turn the gun in my hand, inspecting it.

"What the fuck, Lily?! Where did you get that? Do you even know how to—"

I point the gun above her head at the target in the kitchen, turn the safety off, and pull the trigger. Celeste ducks and quickly turns around to see where I shot. She gets up and stands on the kitchen counter before looking back at me.

"Like I said, I can protect us." I shrug my shoulders, turn the safety back on, and stuff it into the couch. "Jace—" I slam my mouth shut, afraid to tell her. She knows I hate him. I know I hate him, I think... No, I do. I especially hate that he left. "Taught me," I finish.

"Jace taught you?" She crosses her arms as she leans on the counter.

I bring my hand back to my mouth, biting on my nails. Okay, maybe I shouldn't lie, but I can't tell her what happened. I don't know how she will react if she finds out I did things with her boyfriend's coworker. Best friend? No, coworker. Wow, I barely know him. Maybe this empty feeling will be easy to get over then.

"Mhm. Yeah, these past couple of days were kind of hell having him in the house." I shrug my shoulders. "We fought a lot."

I watch her eyes squint as she stares at me.

"Anyway. I took the week off, and I heard you quit your job. So, let's party!"

Celeste drops her arms and her eyes go low.

"Okay maybe not *party* since I have school, but we have a lot more free time! Let's go to Club Opal!"

Celeste shakes her head and starts walking toward the hallway to her room.

"Is that a no?"

Chapter Eight

Jace

♫ "Blind" - Korn ♫

I start my car while waiting for Rowan to get into his after dropping Celeste off. When he called me this morning, he was less than an hour away from the airport to land in New York. He explained to me what his aunt, Alessia, told him in Italy. Now it's time to hunt down everyone if it means finding Joan.

I repeatedly bang my hands on the steering wheel. "Fuck!"

Rowan knocks on my car window, and when I turn to look at him, he gives me a nod and starts heading to his car.

We race through New York traffic, heading to his house. I have my duffle bag with me, but Rowan needs his own.

We slam through his front gate. Rowan's back tires screech to a halt in his driveway. I pull my emergency brake, jumping out of the car and following him up his porch steps.

"Did Alessia tell you where Joan could be?" I ask.

Rowan smacks his front door open, heading straight to his basement. He rushes to unlock all the deadbolts, turning on the lights and going to the wall of weapons.

"Go get me a bag," he demands as he starts removing whatever he deems necessary off the wall.

Joan wasn't just Rowan's mother, but mine as well. We may not be blood but we sure as hell are brothers, whether he sees it like that or not. I grew up not having a mother, forced to live with my shithead father. We lived in the slums because he chose drugs over his own son.

When I met Rowan and went to his house for the first time, his mother saw me, looked me dead in the eyes, and held me. She held me until my lungs felt like they were going to give out. Then she kissed me on top of my head and said, "Welcome to the family." I took that to heart. I was in a family—a family that could possibly love me, cherish me, and choose me. Which she did. I was at their house every day, every night. No questions from Joan. She took me in with open arms.

"Fucking shit, Rowan, can you please tell me what we are doing first?!" I yell as I watch him bring out our biggest weapons. He continues to ignore me while he grabs mags and starts loading the weapons. "I considered her my mother too, ye know," I whisper and turn around to head upstairs for another bag.

When I walk back into the basement, Rowan's hands are grabbing onto the table, his head between his shoulders, looking down at the floor. I stop walking and just watch him, afraid he might crack into pieces.

Three years. We have been searching for Joan for three years and all it took was for her sister to find Rowan and tell him that we fucked up.

I finish walking to him, placing the bag at our feet, and set my hand on his shoulder. "I'm at your side. Whatever we gotta do."

"Then what is holding you back? Pull the fucking trigger if you're such a man," Lance spits.

I stand beside Rowan, watching him point a gun at his father's head as Lance continues to play mind games with him.

"Ye don't even want to explain what happened?" I ask. I have a loaded gun in my waist band, another in my hand, my fingers itching to pull the trigger myself. My vision keeps going dark as my body temperature continues to rise. I don't know if Lance answered my question. I don't know if Rowan asked a question. Every voice seems to mumble past my ears.

My vision clears when I feel something wet splatter on my arm, breaking me out of my trance. I see Rowan on top of Lance, smashing his face into a crimson mess.

"Rowan!" I yell. Now is not the time to kill his father. I won't allow it. I don't have the land, we don't have the right vehicles for transportation, and our clean-up connections aren't in town this week. I wrap my arms around Rowan, pulling him back until we both land on the floor.

Rowan's body shakes as he stares at his father, lying still beside us, possibly lifeless. I get on my feet, walking to Lance. I press two fingers on his neck, feeling a pulse. "We will never get any information from your father if he is dead."

"He's not my father." Rowan stands and walks out of the house.

Six hours, two hundred and forty gallons of gasoline, and a pack of cigarettes later, Rowan and I stand outside of Harper International, watching the flames ignite. Window shards come crashing twelve stories down. It sounds like fireworks as the building starts to collapse.

I jump back into my car, Rowan following. By now, Lance has probably cleaned himself up and we need to go back to his house to gather more information before he tries to flee. If he doesn't want to talk, then I will just let Rowan finish what he started.

"Head for Cold Springs."

"What?" I ask.

"I found John, head for Cold Springs."

I grip the steering wheel as I race us through traffic. Now it's my time to get some built-up anger out. I've been waiting for this day.

I run my hands through my hair. My head is pounding, and I can't stop my body from shaking. This whole feckin' time, the mafia was right under our noses. I sit down on the dusty twin bed in the motel. Rowan asks John questions, but I can't make out anything they are saying. I stopped hearing anything once Rowan said what happened to Joan.

"Why haven't ye killed us?" The words slip from my mouth.

Since the first day John started working with us, I've wanted to kill him. If he is who he says he is, then he wanted to kill us, too. So, what is stopping him? We are here, right in front of him in a shitty motel, in the middle of nowhere.

I turn to Rowan. His face is plastered in bloodstains from Lance. His fingers are twitching, which means there is a good chance he is waiting for the right time to shoot John. When I receive no response to my question, I turn to look at John, seeing him packing clothes into a bag.

I look back at Rowan, widening my eyes to give him the go. We are going to do this. End him here and now before he ends us.

"Don't worry, boys. This ain't over." I notice John reach for a gold ring lying on the dresser. He stuffs it in his pocket and walks out the door.

The worst part about this whole situation is that the mafia used the false identity tactic right under my nose.

The same tactic I use.

Chapter Nine

Lily

♫ "Don't Hurt Yourself (Feat. Jack White)" - Beyoncé♫

I jump on the C-train to Manhattan to catch my 8 a.m. class. Why did I schedule an 8 a.m. class? Let alone an in-person class, one that I could have easily done online? I was praying for a seat on the subway so I could do the reading we were assigned last night, but the train is crammed with people.

We are on our last stop and as I am about to close my book, someone bumps into my back, knocking the book out of my hand. I quickly bend down to pick it up before it gets shredded to pieces by the cockroaches of New York and turn to glare at whoever bumped into me. But as soon as I reach for my book, another hand reaches at the same time.

I look up to see Mateo's brown eyes hiding under circular glasses. His chocolate hair is slicked back, and he is wearing a button-down shirt. From the cut and the stitching, it's not a cheap shirt but a pricey name brand. And those are definitely Saffiano leather loafers.

"Lily. Hi," he says, handing me my book.

I stand up, pushing my book into my chest. "Hi, Mateo." I look around to see everyone getting off the train. "What are you doing here?" I know he works in stocks, or something. So why is he on the subway? I'm sure he makes great money—according to the tips he gives me.

"My car decided not to start today, and I didn't have time to wait to get it fixed."

I nod, as I continue to look around, waiting for space to open so I can get closer to the door when the subway stops.

"New York Practice."

"I'm sorry?" I ask, looking back at Mateo.

"You're studying law?" He points to the book in my hand.

I feel the train jolt and the doors open. I find an opening and squeeze through people heading to the doors. Mateo squeezes right behind me as we get off.

"Um, yeah, at NYU," I say.

"That's awesome. So why are you working at Opal?"

I take my phone out of the back pocket of my jeans, seeing I have less than ten minutes to get to class. "Someone has to pay for my six-figure tuition."

"Well, I'm glad I can help." He winks at me.

I smile at him, walking faster in the direction of campus.

"Let me take you to lunch. Do you have a break between classes?"

I stop in my tracks. I can hear his footsteps stop behind me as well. I knew it was coming. I only have this 8 a.m. class today, but I don't know if I want to tell him that. I tap my fingers on the book crushed into my chest. If I continue telling him no, what if he stops coming to Club Opal? I would be a thousand dollars short each week.

He walks in front of me, lifting his glasses higher on his nose and smiling.

"Okay," I say.

"Good. I will pick you up in front of the school at eleven." He nods and walks in the opposite direction. I pull my phone back out and check the time, now sprinting to campus.

An hour and a half later, I am dazed and starving. My professor returned our issue spotting test, and I got a C-. It's better than an F, I guess. I think about dropping out of law school every day and switching to fashion. My desk drawers at home are filled with drawings and dreams. My closet is packed with scrap materials and my sewing machine. But I am so deep in tuition debt that if I drop out and go into fashion, I will never pay off either one. My debt will die with me. They will bury my bills inside my grave, hoping I will pay them in the afterlife. I will be stuck in this broken down brownstone with Celeste as my roommate for the rest of our lives.

Unless she leaves me for Rowan.

I sit down on a bench outside of campus, looking at my phone. I still have two hours before Mateo meets me. The plan for this lunch is to keep it professional. I do not shit where I eat. I see him for work, he pays me good money to sit at his side and look pretty, and that is it.

Even though he looked incredibly sexy in his glasses with that slicked back hair.

I will not. Fuck. Mateo.

I pull my hood over my hair as the wind starts to pick up, wrapping my arms around my body for warmth. Five years in New York and I'm still not used to this weather. I grab my bag, hoisting it onto my shoulder, and start walking to downtown Manhattan. I could find a place to grab a coffee and start my paper on constitutional law.

I stand in line in a cute little coffee shop. It reminds me of the one I used to work in, but more modern. I show them my NYU ID after ordering to get a discount and walk to an empty table to sit down and wait for my name to be called.

I look around the shop. There are people standing in every corner, waiting for their coffee. I stop and squint when someone catches my eyes. He is wearing a hat, but some of his blonde strands are out, covering most of his forehead and hanging over his sunglasses. He's also wearing a leather blouson and judging by the color and design—a crocodile, lamb, and deerskin mixture—I'm positive I already know whose collection that jacket comes from.

I get out of my seat to start walking toward him. I will pretend to head to the bathroom, but I want to see if I am right regarding the jacket, and I will only know by the little triangle that is stitched on the right-hand side. I like to guess people's outfits. A little game I like to play with myself. Ten times out of ten, I'm usually right, and the closer I get to the mysterious man, the more sure I am of myself. The man pulls his glasses down his nose, his eyes meeting mine and I stop in place.

"Jace?"

His eyebrows pinch together, and he grabs my arm to pull me closer to him. "What are you doing here, *álainn?"* he asks through gritted teeth.

Is he angry at me? Why is he angry at me? He is the one who left without saying "bye" a couple weeks ago, running out of the house to his car as if he was disgusted with me. Like he had somewhere better to be. I can feel the heat on my skin start to rise, the back of my neck breaking out into a sweat.

"I'm getting coffee. What's with the hostility?" I rip my arm out of his grasp. Usually when I have sex with someone, I get a text or a call the next day asking when they can see me again, but I heard nothing from him.

His shoulders straighten, and I have to bend my neck to look up at him. He faces forward, looking out into the crowd of the coffee shop.

"I need you to leave," he says in a dark tone.

I remember Celeste telling me they'd gotten involved with the Italian mafia, but Celeste went on with her life, doing what she always does. She didn't stop her life as if someone were hunting us down. If she doesn't feel any danger, then neither do I.

Jace's head turns to look back down at me, his eyes burning a hole through the lenses of his glasses. What can he do in a coffee shop that would make me feel unsafe?

I hear the bell to the front door of the shop and Jace focuses on the sound, nearly breaking his neck as he puts his head back down to look at his phone. I quickly turn to see who came through the door.

Mateo?

I look over my shoulder at Jace to see he is still pretending to be busy on his phone. I roll my eyes and start walking to Mateo.

"Lily. Hi. What are you doing here?" He lifts his arm to look at his watch. "I was going to pick you up at eleven," he says.

"Yeah. I decided to walk down here and get some coffee beforehand."

He shrugs his shoulders. "Well, that works out then. Did you already order?"

I nod, but then feel a cool chill run down my neck as someone brushes into my shoulder. When I look to the side, I see Jace walking to the front door.

"Well, let me order and we can sit outside and talk," Mateo says.

I keep my eyes on Jace as he walks out of the coffee shop, stopping in front of the window and shaking his head *no*.

What the fuck is going on?

I focus back on Mateo. "Yeah, I will meet you out there." I give him a smile and speed walk to the front door, pushing it open. I feel the wind picking up, blowing my hair into my face. I look to my left and right but don't see Jace anywhere.

The front doorbell chimes again. When I turn around, Mateo is standing there. "Wow, you got yours fast." I say, taking the seat closest to us, pretending I wasn't just standing in one place turning in a circle, looking around like an idiot.

"I'm a regular here."

I smile as he hands me my coffee and takes a seat with me. He removes his glasses, pushing them through his hair. His tan skin looks like he just got back from a vacation in Palm Springs. He covers his wrist with a luxurious watch and his pinky finger is decked in a large medallion ring with a symbol too small for my eyes to make out.

"How was class?" He asks.

My phone vibrates on the table as an unknown number pops up. I look at Mateo and give him an apologetic smile before grabbing my phone, walking away, and bringing it to my ear.

"Hello?"

"Leave."

I pinch my eyebrows and start looking around. I turn back to Mateo and smile at him before walking further away.

"*Álainn,* I need you to walk away. Get back on the subway and go home."

"Jace?" I whisper, shaking my head. "No. I know what happened and why Celeste and Rowan went to Italy. If Celeste isn't stopping her life and hiding, then neither am I."

I can hear that angry grumble through the phone, and it makes my stomach churn in unimaginable ways.

"Please, just do this one thing for me." His voice softens to a whisper.

"What are you going to do, shoot him in front of all these people? He's not in the mafia, Jace. He works in stocks or something." I keep looking at the crowd that surrounds the sidewalks, trying to spot him somewhere. He has to be close if he knows I'm still here with Mateo.

"You don't know him, Lily."

"And I don't know you," I spit.

The line is silent, and when I lift the phone, I see he hung up on me. I raise my head, looking straight in front of me, and see a tall figure on the other side of the street wearing a hat, glasses, and leather jacket. A crowd of people walk past him and when the crowd clears, he's gone.

What type of Joe Goldberg move was that?

I shake my head and walk back to the table. Jace telling me to leave made me a bit nervous, but I don't see an issue with Mateo. He works in stocks, for fuck's sake. Or maybe Jace is jealous—Oh, I can eat that up. He is jealous that Mateo is interested in me and that I am giving him the time of day.

"I'm so sorry, but I must go. Work emergency," Mateo says, holding his phone in the air and shaking it. "Can I drop you off somewhere?"

"Oh no, it's fine. I have errands to run." I lie.

He grabs my hand, lifting it to his mouth, and places a soft kiss on my knuckles. See? Jace has him confused because I see nothing wrong with this man. I am pretty good at reading personalities. I said I never shit where I eat... but maybe I need to let that rule go.

I watch as Mateo stands from his seat and walks toward a car.

Chapter Ten

Lily

♫ "Sex on Fire" - Kings of Leon ♫

I unlock my front door, kicking my shoes off and setting my bag on the counter.

"Why was there a Hippies sandwich under the lamp table?"

I turn around to see Celeste standing there with her arms crossed. I slam my mouth shut as quickly as I open it. I had forgotten to pick it up after everything. I can't even come up with an excuse fast enough that doesn't involve Jace.

Celeste's eyes squint into fine lines, waiting for my response. My fingers find the thread of my shirt, twirling it.

"You know what? Never mind. I have news." she says, unfolding her arms.

I exhale, letting go of the burning breath I was holding as my shoulders fall. "What is it?"

"I met this girl at Central Park, and she just opened an art exhibit down the street. She wants to have an opening with me."

My mouth falls open as Celeste starts smiling. I run to her, smacking us backward on the couch. "Oh my god, Celeste. Congratulations! We are celebrating. Where is the champagne? Pop the bottle!"

I get off the couch, jumping up and down, but notice she is not jumping with me, nor is she smiling. "What's wrong? This is good news, is it not? Why are you not jumping up and down with me?" I puff out my bottom lip while grabbing her shoulders.

"I just— I just haven't heard from Rowan. I saw online that his family business burned down, but since then, he's gone ghost. We left so quick after he spoke to Alessia..."

Wait who is Alessia again?

"And before we left Italy, I found a message in his mother's paintings. I don't know... I'm just scared I fucked up!" Celeste cries.

I grab her, pulling her into my body and hugging her tight. I know she hates touch-y, feel-y me. She always gets so awkward when someone hugs her, but I love her, and she deserves to be hugged.

I feel my shoulder getting wet. "Celeste, you did nothing wrong. I'm sure he just needs some time to get his fucked up, weird life together. He obviously loves you. And if he doesn't, I will shoot him multiple times with Jace's gun," I threaten.

She smacks my arm as she starts to giggle and wipe away her tears.

"C'mon, let's celebrate!" I beg.

"Can't. I have to start working on more paintings." She shrugs, turning on the balls of her heels and running away into her room.

"You suck as a best friend!"

"I love you too!" She yells as she slams her bedroom door and immediately turns on music.

I walk into the pounding sound of some rock band playing. The vibration on the floor permeates my slippers, tickling my toes. Tonight is Purple Nurple—according to my work group chat. All tenders are supposed to be wearing purple. I think the name is hilarious, but Marge disagreed with it, trying to convince us to do any other color or to at least not label it "Purple Nurple."

I take off my coat, hanging it in my locker and grab my purple bedazzled stilettos. I'm wearing a tight leather mini skirt that I made—the color purple, obviously—and I've matched it with a purple lace bralette—that I also made—with a shear light purple shirt on top of it.

I go to the mirrors in the locker room and pull out my purple eyeliner, giving myself an easy little wing.

"I hate this."

I turn to see Rebecca walking in, wearing a tight purple dress that clings to her body, her dark black hair held in a ponytail with a purple scrunchy.

"Purple is so ugly," she finishes.

"No, bitch. You make purple ugly." I put my hand on my hips, looking her up and down. She gives me the middle finger while walking to her locker.

"Have you seen the floor chart?" she asks, sitting on the bench and fixing her shoes.

I turn to my locker, putting my makeup back in my bag. "No, I just got here."

"Purple fucking nurple. What are we, twelve years old?" Marge yells, barging through the door with every other tender who is working tonight. You can tell half of them are already coked out and the other half stumble in drunk. I stand by Rebecca as we wait for Marge to tell us our sections for the night. She names out six other girls and tells them all to get to work.

I grab ahold of Marge's arm before she walks out the door. "Wait! Am I not on the floor?" I ask.

She turns to me with an evil smile. "You've been requested, babe. V I fucking P."

My face falls, my fingernails advancing to my mouth. "Requested by who?"

"I don't know, some Irishman came stomping downstairs after talking to Axel, then Roxxie came by and told me to put you in room five."

Jace.

I have never worked in VIP before. I have delivered drinks to VIP—delivered drinks to Rowan and Jace—but never *worked* VIP. It's fine. Everything is okay. Maybe Rowan is there, and he can explain to me why he hasn't seen Celeste. Or apologize for giving me a babysitter while they were in Italy.

The lights around us dim as the music turns up even louder. I leave my headphones in my locker and walk out the locker room. I stay on the platform that separates the ground level from the VIPs, stopping when I see number five above the red curtains.

I pull the curtain open just enough to slide my body through and see Jace sitting there, working on his laptop with his phone in his other hand.

And no Rowan in sight.

Jace's eyes wander up from his screen, staring directly at me. His eyes are usually a light, piercing blue, but in this light, they are a dark, deep blue like the color of the ocean at night.

"Sit," he commands.

"What do you want, Jace?" I place my hands on my hips, not moving from my spot.

"What's with the hostility, Lily?" He turns his head to the side, mocking my words from the other day when I ran into him at the coffee shop.

I twist my arms along my chest and slowly sit down, just feet away from him at the end of the leather sectional. He stands from his seat, walking toward me. I press my knees together, my body setting itself on fire at his height, his eyes, his hair, his smell... his everything. Ever since that one night at the house, everything about him makes my body feel like I'm being burned by a thousand matches. I straighten my back against the couch when his hand comes up to my face, pushing my hair behind my ear.

"No headphones today, *álainn*?"

"Nope. I thought Rowan would be here to apologize. Wanted to make sure I heard him clearly," I state.

He scoffs and moves back to sit at his computer. "Rowan doesn't apologize."

"Does Jace apologize?" I ask.

His head snaps up in my direction, tipping his chin down while his eyebrows lower. "Apologize for what?"

"I know it is, like, an *Irish* thing to do—" A half snort, half laugh leaves his lips as he leans back, putting his arms above the couch and spreading his legs. I bite my lower lip and keep my eyes on his face, focusing on not looking at anything lower than his chest. "To leave without saying bye. But it was kind of a dick move after what happened," I finish saying.

With the blink of an eye, he moves to my side. His hand is back at my face as he uses one finger to slowly draw a line from my nose, over my lips, to the middle of my chest. I keep my head held up, staring at him.

"After what, Lily?" he asks, deepening his accent.

My breath catches as his finger glides down to my nipple. He pinches one and I bite my lower lip, from letting any type of sound come from my mouth.

"I can't stay here," I breathe out.

"You can and you will."

"We don't take tips from VIPs, and I need the money."

His hand falls from touching me as he leans back. His jaw pulses and his hands ball into fists. "You're not going back on that floor."

"You can't tell me what to do!" I stand from the couch, pacing around the room. "First it was the command to leave the coffee shop and now you're trying to control me and my job?! What was your issue at the shop anyway?" I snap.

"Every night you work... I will be here. And you will be in this room with me," he states calmly.

I run my fingers through my hair. God, he doesn't get it. He doesn't understand. I *need* to be on the floor. I take a deep inhale, closing my eyes so I don't lash out any more than I need to. "Jace... those tips keep me in college. Wait..." I turn to face him. "You didn't answer my question about the coffee shop. Are you trying to keep me away from Mateo?"

I watch as his head snaps back in my direction, his pupils getting smaller like a cat searching for its prey. I jump onto the couch, sitting on my knees. "Oh my god, Jace Cook, are you jealous?" I question, waving my finger at him.

"Don't call me that," he grits, turning back to work on his laptop.

"Call you what?" I ask, my smile falling from my face.

"Cook."

I don't understand. Is that not his name? Whatever. I am over this. Over him. He may not be a stalker like his buddy Rowan, but he sure as fuck is a control freak. I remove my legs from under me, sitting normally on the couch, looking around. I can't be on the floor today since my section is being taken care of. So now I am stuck staring at this tacky room—red leather sectional, a little black table in the middle, red curtains, red walls. Red everything. I know this club's income is better than this.

"What am I supposed to do?" I lean my head back, staring at the ceiling.

"Do what you always do at work," he responds, his fingers tapping against his keyboard. "Which is what, Mister Know-It-All?"

He stops typing, turning to look at me. "Sit there and look pretty."

"Boooring. At least my customers would dish juicy gossip," I say, scooting closer to him and trying to peek at his computer. It looks like the same green screen and random symbols that pops up on my computer at home all the time. Weird. "What are you doing?" I ask.

"Classified."

I roll my eyes, standing from the couch. "I'm going to go get a drink."

"Bring a bottle," he says.

Heading for the curtain, I sarcastically ask, "Anything else, Your Highness?"

His eyes leave his computer screen as he gives me a devilish grin, his sharp canines protruding from his lips. I can feel the blood rush from my cheeks down to my neck. "Don't answer that," I quickly say, stepping around the curtains and heading down the stairs off the platform. I look around the club to see it's packed. Every seat, every couch, is filled. I notice a couple tenders sitting on laps, some giving massages to crusty men, bending to show their goods to the other men sitting behind them.

My eyes scan my normal section to see if I can spot any familiar faces, but nobody looks recognizable. This is going to be a long fucking night.

I make my way toward the back of the club to the liquor room. As soon as I crack the door open, a hand slams it shut. I quickly turn around to see Mateo in an all-black suit. His eyes are squinted, which is a sign that he is already highly intoxicated.

"I've been looking everywhere for you, gorgeous."

"Hi, Mateo," I say, giving him a tight smile.

Mateo gets a bit touchy when he is drunk. I always try to leave early when he gets this way. He is a nice guy. I've never had major issues with him, but I'm starting to get this eerie feeling in the pit of my stomach. Maybe I'm overthinking it too much. Maybe Jace fried my brain with his non-answers. Or maybe the "don't shit where you eat" voice is telling me this is a bad idea.

Oh my god, I cannot make my mind up with this man!

He takes a step back, giving us space. "Where have you been? I've been waiting for you."

"Yeah, sorry, I was requested in VIP," I say.

I watch his eyes light up like a kid in a candy store. Anytime someone is specifically requested for VIP, it is assumed she is giving the *full* VIP package. Sex and whatnot. Which is not true. We have a voice here. We can say who and what we are willing to do. Axel gives us a choice, and my choice will always be no. Anytime a girl gets uncomfortable in VIP, there is a little button we can press. Once that button is pressed, security comes ripping apart the man in the room and he is banned for life. I have seen it happen once or twice. Aaron, our security guard, will come strutting out of the dark like a shadow in the night, rip open the curtain, and shove his fist into someone's face. They leave with broken noses or jaws one hundred percent of the time.

I take a step back, reaching behind me to grab the door handle. He must pick up on my nervousness and drops his eyes, shoving his hands in his front pockets.

"I feel like we never got to finish our coffee. Can we try again?"

"Um, yeah, sure. I'm just pretty busy with school and work most of the time, but—"

Jace appears out of thin air, stepping in front of Mateo and pushing me back further into the door. His chest heaves and his eyes penetrate through me like lightning.

"I'm waiting." His hands clench and unclench at his sides.

Seriously? What is his fucking issue tonight?

"I'm tending to another customer right now," I whisper in his face, pointing behind him where he's clearly ignoring the other man standing right behind him.

Mateo coughs lightly into his hand, bringing himself to attention. Jace ignores the sign and leans further into me, his lips brushing against my ear, and I can feel the bulge at his center pressing against my stomach. I really hope that's just a gun in his pants and not his—

"If I remember correctly, VIP means VIP *only*. You tend to *me* only," he grits out.

My thoughts are cut off at the sound of his gravelly voice so close to my skin, his scent so prominent and unique.

"It's good to see you, Jace," Mateo interrupts. "How's work?"

Jace leans back, squinting his eyes at me. He barely turns his head over his shoulder, never breaking our contact, and says, "Mr. Davenport, always lovely to see you."

Mr. Davenport? So Jace does know him? And he was trying to keep me away from him at the coffee shop? Jace finally turns around, extending his hand to shake Mateo's. His grumpy, controlling attitude turns off like a light switch, his accent prominent once more, and you can feel the energy change around him.

"Obviously, there is some *tending* that is requested." Mateo waves his hand between me and Jace. "So, I will let you guys get back to it." He shoves his hands back into his pockets before giving us a smile and nod, and walks away.

I shove on Jace's back, hoping he will tip over, but his body barely rocks. "You're fucking with my money, Mr. Cook!"

I push him again because I can. Because he is fucking infuriating. Because he is possibly fucking with my love life. We had one night together. One fucking amazing, orgasmic night together, and now he thinks he owns me? Controls me? I hate that anytime I am around him, my body lights up like fireworks, but my brain melts with hatred.

He watches as Mateo disappears into the crowd in the club. His head turns over his shoulder, not fully looking at me as he says, "Bring something expensive."

Chapter Eleven

Lily

♬ "Stupid Girl" - Garbage ♬

He wanted the most expensive bottle, so I sold him the most expensive bottle. I had to grab a ladder from the supply closet just to reach it on the highest shelf. "Remy Martin Cognac Louis XIII," I read off the label. I have never tasted it, nor even thought about putting my hands on something like this. I had to notify Roxxie about the sale for Axel to clear it in the computer and put it on Jace's tab.

Back in the section, I slam the bottle on the table next to him and sit my ass down on the other side of the sectional.

We don't speak to each other for the rest of the night. He sits there on his computer, typing away and running his hands through his hair like a fucking manic while drinking straight from the bottle.

I keep myself entertained with my cuticles, making a mental note to bring nail supplies on my next shift just in case I'm stuck with him again.

By the time he is done with whatever keeps him busy on his computer, he packs up his laptop, shoves it in his arms, stands and walks out the section, saying absolutely nothing to me. He drank half the bottle and yet does not stumble, fumble, or trip when he walks out of the room. I don't understand how he is not completely intoxicated. My stomach churns at the thought of him getting behind the wheel.

Finally, I force my stiff body off the couch and make my way to the locker room. I look at the clock on the wall and note it's almost three in the morning. The lights are slowly starting to brighten throughout the club, and I can hear people stumbling and laughing on their way to the exits.

"How was your first VIP?" Marge walks in, grabbing cash from out of her bra.

"I'd rather shove my own foot in my throat next time," I say, ripping off my heels and throwing them into my locker.

She stops moving, her eyes bulging. "Oh my, he had a foot fetish?" she asks, crinkling up her nose in disgust.

I chuckle only because I can see Jace having some type of fetish. I wouldn't put it past him to like sucking on toes.

"No, I'd just rather be on the floor than be stuck in confinement again. It was prison," I say.

"Go talk to Axel."

I laugh harder this time, throwing my head back and wiping away the tears falling down my cheeks as I try to catch my breath. I look back at Marge to see her standing there, her eyebrows reaching her hairline and her hands on her hips.

"Nobody talks to Axel, Marge. Isn't that what you said?"

"True," she states, counting her money. "But if you seriously don't like it, you tell Roxxie, and because it's a VIP, she is forced to take you to Axel for the situation."

My face falls, throat tightening at the thought of meeting Axel. I have worked here for over three years and never met the man who writes my checks. Never put a face to the name. Never heard the voice of the man who makes millions a year from millionaires.

Marge shrugs her shoulders at me, walking to her locker. "I'm just giving you an option, sweetheart. Don't start having a panic attack over it."

"Have you ever met Axel?" I whisper.

She nods. "Yeah. Once, four years ago. I was uncomfortable with a VIP. He never did anything but would say degrading shit to me. I didn't think it was enough to get him kicked out completely, I just never wanted to be in that room with him again. One stop to Axel's office and it was done." She looks up at the ceiling, placing her fingertips on her chin. "Come to think about it though, I never saw his face. When I walked in, his chair was facing that large window that looks down at the club. He stayed facing away from me the entire time. Roxxie was in the room, too. She spoke for him. So I never heard his voice either." She shrugs her shoulders again, picking up her purse from the bench.

I twirl my finger in my shirt, thinking about meeting my big bad boss for the first time ever.

I pluck off the note taped to my bedroom door.

Mark the date, June 6th art exhibit.

I squeal reading Celeste's handwriting. I couldn't be more proud of her. Opening my bedroom door, I tape the note to my computer and throw myself onto my bed. My conversation with Marge replays in my head. I'm trying to find the pros of being in VIP with Jace. Fortunately, I don't find any. They are all cons. If I stay in VIP with him, he will annoy me, try to control me, won't let me talk to anyone else, and most of all, I won't make any money. I still owe seventy-seven grand on my school tuition this year, which will only increase for the next three semesters. I shouldn't have quit Caffee Latte, but Jace sticking up for me opened my eyes to the emotional and mental abuse I was going through with my boss. It's too late now, though. I doubt I would be hired again after Jace picked my boss up by the throat and practically threatened to kill him.

Ever since Rowan forced him to come babysit me, it's like he has this protective instinct over me. Maybe I can talk to Rowan and tell him to put his dog on a leash or a shock collar. Rowan needs to tell him, "Bad dog, leave the poor girl"—a.k.a. me—"alone."

That's if we ever see Rowan again. Celeste told me she hasn't talked to him since Italy. I should have asked Jace about that. I shake my head at the fact that I'm a terrible friend. Okay, I will handle one more VIP for one night just so I can freaking ask Jace where the fuck Rowan is and tell him to stop fucking around with Celeste. She is wife material and deserves the world.

I scrape myself off the bed after having my mental conversation with myself and head for the shower so I can get ready for bed.

I walk out of my criminal law class, squeezing between people so I can quickly catch the subway back home.

Criminal law is my least favorite. If I ever finish school before I drop dead, I will refuse to be a defense attorney. I'd rather work in family law than have to deal with criminals all day. My best friend dealing with a boyfriend who is possibly being hunted by the mafia is enough drama for me.

"Lily!"

I stop walking, turning around and scanning the crowd. I swear I heard my name, but nobody around me is staring at me or looks remotely familiar. Ignoring it, I take two steps to continue walking when someone pulls my hand back. I flip around to see Mateo behind me. I rip my hand back and clutch my books into my chest.

"Sorry. I didn't mean to pull your hand like that. I've just been—" He wipes his hand across his forehead. "I've been waiting for you to get out of class. I wasn't sure if you had class or not today so I've kind of been waiting all day," he says, his cheeks turning a shade of pink.

I stare at him in shock. He's wearing a two-piece dark blue plaid suit, those cute little glasses, and his hair is a little ruffled from either his hands or the wind.

I hold out my hand to him and his eyes dart down, looking confused. I shake my hand and say, "Hand me your phone."

He pulls his phone out of his front pocket and puts it in my hand. I swipe up to find it unlocked and enter my phone number, handing it back to him. "There. You have my number and now you don't have to wait. Text next time."

His smile reaches his eyes as he nods, staring at his phone like I handed him gold. "Want to take a walk with me?"

I pull my phone out of my back pocket to look at the time. Shit. "I'm sorry," I say as I start skipping backward. "I have to make the subway to get home."

"I'll take you home," he spits out quickly.

I stop moving, staring at him. If he takes me home, then he will know where I live and where I work. If he knows where I live, then there is a possibility he could be a psycho and show up anytime he wants. Or he could rob us, or hire someone to rob us. Or kill us. Kill me! Most psychopaths pretend to be really nice in the beginning before they murder their victims and then throw them in a freezer. Or a lake. Or an ocean. Or a dump site!

If a psychopath shows you they are crazy from the start, does that mean they are not actually psychos? I mean, Jace and Rowan are both a little crazy. Rowan was stalking Celeste—we don't count Celeste following him home, she was doing her job. Rowan always knew where she was. Had keys to the house and probably has cameras in her room like a weirdo. Jace almost killed my boss for me, showed me how to use a gun, somehow got my cell phone number, and is trying to be controlling, all within a couple of days of getting to know me outside my job.

"Okay." I shrug my shoulders, letting the overthinking roll off me.

If he kills me, I won't be an attorney. I won't have to go through the absolute heartbreak of telling my parents I dropped out of law school. Instead, they will have to deal with burying their oldest daughter. Little depressing, but I would rather die than break my parents' hearts.

"Great," he says, smiling and throwing his arm over my shoulder.

Chapter Twelve

Jace

♫ "Something in the Way" - Nirvana ♫

Are you feckin' kidding me? He waited all day at NYU for Lily? We have been here since 8 a.m. It's now 12 p.m. I jump out of my car, pulling my hood over my head and face.

I told Lily to stay away from him. I need her to stay away from.

I follow them down the street, heading to downtown Manhattan. They stop at some bakery, heading inside. I don't know how to get it through her beautiful blonde hair to her feckin' noggin' to stay away from him.

She should probably stay away from me too, but I like looking at her. I liked her being in the VIP room with me. The whole time, she thought I was focused on my laptop, but I couldn't focus one feckin' bit. I was typing nonsense while stealing glances at her the whole time. Her strawberry scent kept blowing straight to me with the AC. Her big green eyes stared down at her hands—and that purple outfit... feckin' *bollocks* I wanted to rip it off her. Then she left the room to get drinks, and I wanted to rip my clothes off and hand them to her so nobody would look at her. I could only contain myself for two minutes before I followed her out of the section to make sure nobody was bothering her. I stayed back, pretending I wasn't following her, until I saw Mateo.

My eyes stay planted on the window to the bakery they've decided to stop at. I take a random seat across the street, watching her laugh, throwing her head back. She swipes her hair off her shoulder and takes her jacket off, showing off her porcelain skin. I groan. I think about how possible it would be for me to shoot through the bakery window and put a bullet in the middle of his forehead without hitting any other civilians. If I walked in right now, and sliced his throat with my knife, how much blood would stain her beautiful face? Would she be scarred for life? Would she hate me for traumatizing her? For scaring her?

"What can I get you, sir?"

I look up from under my hood to see a waitress holding a notepad out. When I turn around in my seat to see where I am, I realized I've sat in another bakery. Who puts this many bakeries on one street?

"Just so you know, we close in about twenty minutes," the waitress states, chewing hard on the gum in her mouth and blowing a bubble.

I quickly look at the menu. "An everything bagel, toasted twice, cream cheese, lots. And put shoes on it."

The waitress nods as I hand her the menu. I turn my head to see Lily and Mateo have moved outside with coffee cups. I clench my fingers around the table as she laughs again at something he said.

What is so funny to her? What charms does he use to make her shine brighter than a star at night? Why does my *álainn* woman think it is okay to just trust any man? Trust anyone? Not in this century. Not in this world. She should trust no one. Not even me. How can I ever focus on this case when she continues to insert herself into everything?

Rowan has been working from home. Hasn't left his house in days, months, and right now, I could really use him. Following Mateo for the past couple of days has truly been a pain. His ex-wife is missing—missing a little too well. It's super easy for us to track significant others, but when they are missing to the point where *we* can't find them, the case becomes an issue. Then we have to start looking into the X factor—the husband. Mateo is pushing all the wrong and right buttons. He keeps quiet, clean on all his ends, but why would he hire us to find his wife just to serve her divorce papers and get a family heirloom? Most men want their money back or try to bribe us to *take out* the wife for extra money.

Which never happens. We don't kill women. And when a customer asks us to do that, we kill them instead.

Most of the men who go to Club Opal are under Axel's protection, Mateo being one of them. Luckily, I was able to make a deal with Axel for Rowan and me—when that feckin' *gobshite* decides to come out of hiding—to make a move on Mateo.

"You can sit here but I need to close your tab." The waitress hands me a bag of my food and my check. I pull out my wallet and hand her a hundred-dollar bill.

"Keep the change," I say, grabbing the bag when I see Mateo and Lily start getting out of their seats.

I continue to follow them from the opposite sidewalk and stop when I see him open the passenger door of his car for her. If I pull out my phone right now and call her, she will know I am watching her. She is getting herself into something she doesn't want to be involved in. I refuse to let her be blind like we were with the Rossis. I have a feeling in my gut that something is not right, and I refuse to ignore it.

I jump into my car parked directly across from his and follow Mateo's blacked out BMW. We drive all the way back to Lily's house. She gets out the car, waves goodbye to him, and heads inside.

I pull into a parking spot a few cars down. Mateo is still pulled to the side of the road, waiting, even though Lily is already inside. People fill the streets and the sun is at its peak. If I am going to do this, I need to make it fast.

I hop out my car, keep my head down, and cross the street. The universe decides to work with me today—A kid runs up to Mateo's car and knocks on his window. I hear the kid ask if he wants to buy some chocolate when I reach the trunk of Mateo's car. I pull my tracker out of my pocket and bend down to place it underneath his car as I simultaneously pretend to drop my phone. I continue walking down the alley behind Lily's house, dragging her neighbor's trash can with me.

Let's find out where you are hiding your wife, Mr. Davenport.

Chapter Thirteen

Lily

♫ "I Hate Everything About You" - Three Days Grace ♫

Mateo offered me a job—like a big-girl, grown-up job. As a paralegal. At a law firm in his office building. A. Big. Girl. Job.

When he dropped me off, I told him I would think about it. It pays well, I could work there during the day and pick up random shifts at the club at night. My only hesitation is if I take this job, I feel I would be drifting further away from the idea of being a fashion designer. Taking the job would mean being in law school is purposeful and not a waste of my time.

I hear the front door open and look down the hallway to see Celeste coming through the door. She walks into the kitchen, grabbing two bowls and cereal. I get up from the couch to sit at the kitchen island. She pours us both a bowl and slides one in front of me. "You got my note, right?" she asks.

"July seventh. I'm so excited!" I say, shoving a spoon into my mouth.

"It's June sixth." Celeste puts her hands on her hips, tilting her head to the side.

"Shit. Sorry, yes. I still have the sticky note. It's on my computer. I hope you don't mind I invited everyone I know in my class and someone from the club."

"Who from the club?"

I press my tongue against my teeth before whispering, "Mateo."

Her eyes widen as she takes a seat next to me. "Mateo. The one who throws money at you, Mateo?"

I nod my head in confirmation.

"What happened to 'you don't shit where you eat'?!"

I shove another spoonful of cereal into my mouth. "I never said I slept with him," I say, spitting cereal at her.

"Not yet," she snarks.

I hit her on the arm with the back of my hand. "Hey, I have some morals."

"Oh yeah? So, what happened with you and Jace when I was gone?"

I choke on my cereal, feeling the marshmallows and milk go down the wrong tube. Celeste lays her head in her hand that is propped up on the counter while I pound on my chest.

When I finally catch my breath, I say, "Nothing," and shake my head.

"Don't forget I fell for his best friend. I remember all the cues and the way I acted." She points at me, obviously referencing the coughing fest I just had. "They are different," she whispers under her breath.

"No. What they are is crazy."

"True." She shrugs, finishing her cereal and throwing it into the kitchen sink before heading to her side of the house.

I look at my phone when I hear a ping.

Reminder: Gala

I jump out of my chair, screaming and grabbing my bowl of cereal to run to my room. I turn on my computer, going straight to the live stream. Every year, the gala is held here in New York City, a little over an hour away from my house. And every year I cry my eyes out on the fact that my dress is not being worn on the red carpet.

I shove another spoonful of cereal into my mouth as I watch the rest of the celebrities sway onto the red carpet. My cheeks turn cold as I feel wet drops run down them. I put my bowl to the side, pulling my knees to my chest, and stare at the drawer that my sketchbook is shoved into.

I open the drawer, gathering the courage to pull out the book, and open it to the first page. A couple of years ago, I drew an all-black jumpsuit with white crisscross stitching. The arms are long, cut at a diagonal to give it a fairy look, and the chest is a low-cut V, pinched at the waist with bell bottom pants. I flip to the next page—a short, tight black dress with long sleeves but the shoulders are pinched large, giving it a *Cruella de Vil* look, crested with rhinestones and diamonds at the square neck.

I'm going to make this, and I am going to wear it to Celeste's art exhibit.

I walk into the club earlier than usual today. It smells like lavender, meaning the carpets have been freshly vacuumed. The lights are still bright, and no music has started playing, giving me a little peace so I can gather my thoughts and focus on my plan here.

I spot a short, tan shadow lurking in the back of the club. "Roxxie!" I scream, jogging to her and stopping right in her path.

She looks me up and down, her facial muscles not moving an inch.

"You like? I made it myself." I hold my arms out and give her a spin. Today I'm wearing a leather pink dress I made. It has the illusion of belts wrapping all along it. One belt is holding my tits together, tightly.

"Not particularly. What can I do for you, Miss Ballis?"

My smile falls, but I hold my chin up high. "I need to speak to Axel." I decide my best friend will just have to hate me because I will not be stuck in VIP today.

"Reason?" Roxxie asks.

"Reason... I—" I look around me to see if any other tenders are peeking around the corner. Anytime someone mentions Axel's name, everyone wants the tea, and I am not about to be put in the middle of some fake rumor or drama.

"I have a concern with a VIP," I whisper.

"Follow me," she snaps, turning on her heels like a drill sergeant. She pulls back the red rope, allowing me to walk up the flight of stairs. At the top is a long hallway with multiple doors. She opens the first one on the left and allows me to step in. I look around the large all-black room. The floors are marbled black, the walls are black. No paintings. No decorations. Just one desk, one laptop and three chairs. The lighting is dim, and the air is freezing cold.

I bet taking a nap in here is peaceful.

The chair behind the desk is facing out the window that shows the whole bottom floor of the club. I stand near the door as Roxxie walks up to the chair behind the desk, bending down to whisper.

"What?" Roxxie snaps, standing up straight. Her lips curve downward, and she crinkles her nose like she's smelled something horrendous.

So she does have facial muscles?!

Her head turns toward me, then back to Axel, nodding once. My throat closes as I watch her stomp my way. Did I say something wrong? Why is she walking toward me? What did Axel say? Am I being fired? What if he already knows what is going on? All he does is sit in this office all day, watching everyone below him like some Greek god.

"Move," Roxxie demands, standing right in front of my face.

I whip around, grabbing the door handle, and scurry out of the office. When I turn back around, Roxxie is still standing in the room.

"Are you going to talk to him or not?" She points over her shoulder to one of the chairs behind her, in front of Axel's desk.

I widen my eyes, looking between her and the back of Axel's chair, then make an 'o' with my lips. I slowly walk into the office and sit in the chair at the front of his desk. My body jumps at the sound of the door slamming behind me. I turn my head over my shoulder to see Roxxie no longer in the room.

Lord, if I make it out alive from this meeting, I promise not to drink... I'll settle down in a white picket fence house... I'll go to church—

"VIP, huh?"

My jaw drops when the chair turns around to show me the man sitting in front of me. I quickly close my mouth, darting my eyes around the office. When I turn my gaze back to him, he stares at me, leaning back in his chair. He has two different colored eyes. One of them looks black and the other eye is half black, half blue. His dark hair is messy, cut into a modern mullet. He has naturally tan skin with big pouty lips and a goatee, and the sound of his voice is like silk. Is this why nobody is ever allowed to see him? Because he could make anyone purr like a needy cat? If any of the girls in this club saw him, they would be jumping his bones. Me included. Sign me up. Fuck my "don't shit where you eat" rule.

"Yes," I cough up, slamming my eyes tight at the sound of my own voice. I sound like a twelve-year-old boy going through puberty in front of my very sexy boss. "Yes, I um... need to be on the floor."

"Why?" he asks, leaning his elbows on his desk and interlocking his fingers.

"I like walking around and interacting with people." I pull my shoulders back and lift my head up. I practiced this all night. I need to show my dominance and put my foot down.

He huffs, or maybe hums. Or was it a fucking chuckle? I don't even know, but I can feel my sweat start to pile up near my hairline. I have strands sticking to the back of my neck and I'm rubbing my fingers raw on this leather chair.

"You are one of my top employees here, which shows on your paychecks. Does it not?" he questions.

"Yes sir, it's just that—" I close my mouth before I finish that sentence. I hate telling people I am in school. I hate telling people I need more money to afford to live in a brownstone with a roommate and go to law school. I don't want to be a seventy-five-year-old piled up in debt because I couldn't tell my parents the truth. "I have regulars who always request me. I don't want to disappoint them." I can feel my eye twitch at the lie. This was not the dialogue I had planned in my head.

A smile breaks on Axel's face, but not a sweet, lovely smile. It's a smile that hyenas make when they are chasing their meal. He stands from his chair, and I notice his plain white T-shirt, dark jeans, and converse. For a man who makes millions, he sure doesn't dress like it.

I tilt my head to the sky, because of course he towers over me. He stops walking and sits on top of his desk in front of me, our knees only inches apart, forcing me to push my chair back to give him some more leg space.

"You know, I am not a huge fan of liars."

"I am not lying. I do have regulars—"

"But that's not the reason you don't want to be in VIP. You're a smart girl, in law school, live in a decent home," he interrupts.

Wait, how does he know all of this?

"Understand this, Miss Ballis, I can respect a bad decision, but I can't respect a liar. So, I'll ask you again. Why don't you want to be in the VIP section?"

The taste of iron fills my mouth as I bite at my cheek. I take a moment before saying, "Being on the floor helps pay for school and—" I exhale, letting my shoulders fall. "Jace irritates me."

A full laugh comes from the pit of Axel's chest as he throws his head back. When he finishes laughing at whatever he thought I said was funny—because I was not joking—he uses his fingers to pinch my chin before standing up and walking back behind his desk to sit in his chair. I can feel my cheeks heat at the action he just did.

"Jace irritates everyone." He interlocks his fingers again on his desk, leaning forward. "Now, if it's money you are worried about, your school has already been funded for this year. If you need more, I can raise your paycheck to seventy-five dollars an hour but unfortunately, there—"

"Wait!" I interrupt, shaking my head and trying to rewind in my head what he just said. "I'm sorry, did you say my school was funded? I don't understand."

Axel squints his eyes, creating three deep lines on his forehead. He opens his laptop, typing, and turns the screen around for me to see my school account. Details show that seventy-seven thousand dollars was paid three days ago, and my current balance is zero.

Starring at the screen, I start babbling, "Did you pay for this? I can pay you back. I don't understand. How did you even—"

He shakes his head back and forth, turning his laptop back to him. "I'm guessing Jace didn't inform you of this decision? He requested you be in VIP every time he is here. Now, I prefer my women happy and comfortable. I know being in VIP means walking home with no cash. So, as a result of you tending him every night with no cash, he offered to pay for your schooling and made me a business deal."

I can feel my heart beating out of my chest. I told Jace about me needing tips in private. I wasn't asking for a fucking handout. I don't need his help.

"I can still raise your paychecks, but I would need you to sign a new contact. I know Jace can be... interesting. But if there is no abuse—mentally, physically, or spiritually—I cannot have you back on the floor. I will need you in VIP until Jace requests otherwise. If he does decide to break the rules that he specifically knows of, or abuses this power, then you advise me, and I can make him disappear. Otherwise, have a good shift, Miss Ballis."

As soon as he says my name, the door to his office opens behind me. Roxxie stands there, waiting for me to exit. I look back at Axel, his arms crossed against his chest, and he gives me a slight nod. I stand and walk out, passing Roxxie and going straight to the stairs.

I was in Axel's office for less than half an hour. The music is already blasting, and we have a full house. Some girls are dragging men behind curtains, while others walk the floor with bottles in hand. I zone out everything around me, my ears tuning out the music as I walk straight toward the locker room, needing to change into my heels.

"Hey baby, I didn't see you at roll call," Marge says, coming out of the liquor room holding two bottles.

"I was meeting with Axel."

She follows me into the locker room. I open my locker and take off my slippers, sitting on the bench to lace up my heels.

"By the way you are slamming things... I'm assuming the meeting didn't go well?"

I look around to see other tenders standing near the mirrors, adding layers of makeup.

"I'll talk to you later," I whisper and give Marge a hesitant smile. I close my locker shut, turn the lock, and walk out the room straight to the platform. I rip open the curtain to room five and find Jace in the same spot as last time with his head in his computer. I stomp my feet on the ground all the way toward him. As soon as he lifts his head to look at me, I raise my hand and slap him across the face.

Chapter Fourteen

Lily

♫ "Glory Box" - Portishead ♫

My body freezes as I stare at Jace. I can't believe I just did that. He rolls his neck back to me slowly. My eyes zone in on his mouth as his tongue swipes the crimson off his bottom lip. I slowly start to back away, my heart battering against my chest. He stands from his seat, towering almost two feet over me. I continue walking backward until I fall onto the couch.

He plants his hands right above my head on the sofa. "Any particular reason you decided to be violent today, *álainn?*"

As soon as I open my mouth the speak, he leans closer to me, swiping his tongue over my lips. I can taste the iron that lingers, electricity streaming down to the pit of my stomach, I close my eyes to take a deep breath, washing away the emotion. Exchanging my lust to anger, I lift my arms, pushing him on his chest, but he doesn't back away. I push again and again until he finally releases the death grip he has on the couch. He backs away, letting me stand up. I go to open my mouth, but it feels as if I have a hand crushing my windpipe. My eyes burn, and there's pressure in my ears. I blink fast and hard to clear my vision. "My situation was private," I whisper.

"Specifics, *álainn.*"

I close my eyes, "My school. You paid for my fucking school! Is this some sort of game? You babysit me once and now you think you have control of me? You say who I can and can't hang out with and what I'm allowed to do and not do?! Now you pay for my school! For what?! So I'd feel bad and continue to stay in VIP for you?"

"I don't see an issue here," he deadpans.

I start pacing around the room, running my hands through my hair. "Resolute. Have you ever heard of the term before, Mr. Cook? It means—" I'm cut off when he pulls my arm backward, crashing my body into him.

"I told you not to call me that," he sneers. His face is only inches from mine. I watch as he drags his eyes from mine down to my lips, his sharp eyes turning soft as he loosens his grip on my arm.

"What is your issue?!" I push him off me, causing me to fall back onto the couch. I prop my elbows on my knees, wiping my hands down my face. I watch as Jace starts to walk away, pulling the curtain back. "Hey! Where are you going?! We are not finished here!"

He turns his head over his shoulder, thinning his lips he says, "The *jacks*," and closes the curtain behind him.

The jacks? What does that even mean?

I throw my head back against the couch, staring at the ceiling. Now what am I going to do? How am I supposed to pay him back? Maybe I can take Mateo's job offer. Work there from nine to five then be at the club by nine at night. It's like when I was working at Caffee Latte, except I will have shorter nap times in the afternoon and will have to work on school... When I can.

I stand from the couch, peeking my head out of the curtain and looking around. No Irish man in sight, but I do spot Mateo.

I walk toward him and his friends who are sitting in the middle section of the club. "Hi, Mateo."

His eyes are barely open as he looks me up and down, scanning my body like a prized possession. Suddenly, I'm feeling very naked.

"Well, hey there, pretty girl. I've missed you. Sit down with me."

I look around us, scanning the crowd. "Um, I can't. I just wanted to let you know I would like that interview, for what you offered."

His smile reaches his eyes as he stands, holding out his hand. "Great, you're hired."

"I'm sorry? I thought—"

"You're hired. That was your interview. I'll text you the address and details," he whispers into my ear over the loud music.

I scratch my forehead, not understanding how that was an interview. "I—"

"Miss Ballis."

I turn around to see our bodyguard, Aaron, standing behind me. He's as wide as a linebacker, but shorter than me when I'm wearing heels.

"You're requested back in your room."

I roll my eyes, turning back to Mateo. He gives me a nod and turns to sit back on the couch with his friends.

Now we are sending other people to fetch me? This is fucking fantastic. It's like he has never left my side since Rowan and Celeste went to Italy.

I rip the curtains open, seeing nobody in the room. His laptop is gone, and everything is cleared off the table. I turn back around to see Aaron standing guard.

"Where is he?"

"Who, ma'am?" Aaron asks.

"Jace?"

Aaron looks to his left and right in confusion.

"Jace, the one who is always in room five. Annoying Irish dude. Tall, blonde hair, eyes like a husky. Jace!" I scream, getting irritated with this whole ordeal.

"I'm not sure, Miss Ballis, I was told to keep you in room five."

"Why? By who? Nobody is even here!"

"I am just doing my job."

If I could scream and throw a tantrum right now, I would, but he is right. He is just doing his job, and I cannot blame him for it. It's not his fault. It's Jace's.

I give him a tight smile, calming myself down, and close the curtain in front of me.

"Stop, Celeste," I mumble, feeling my body jerked multiple times. "Five more minutes." I turn my body, snuggling my arms into my chest. I feel my legs being dragged off the bed. "Oh my god!" I whip my head around and scream when I see Roxxie standing in front of me.

I take in my vicinity and see I am still at work.

"It's after hours. You need to leave."

"I am so sorry." I gather myself, wiping the dried-up crust I feel near the corner of my mouth. I stand, running out of the room to the lockers. I look at the clock to see it's past 4 a.m. Did Jace ever come back? Why wouldn't he wake me if he did? I switch from my heels to my slippers, grabbing my bag and heading out the front door.

The sun is barely rising and the cool morning breeze brushes past my legs, causing a shiver throughout my body. I pull my bag off my shoulder to pull out my trench coat, wrapping it tightly around myself. I walk out of the alley into the main road, spotting a taxi. I wave my hand in the air to try and get his attention, but the stupid yellow car decides to ignore me and drives past. This would be a really nice time to have a car. Luckily, there is another one coming. I wave my hand in the air again, hoping to catch this one.

My whole body jumps when I hear a high-pitched whistle right behind me. I turn around to see Mateo removing his two fingers from his mouth. When I turn back around, the taxi is pulling to the curb.

"I thought whistling for taxis only works in movies."

"Yeah, well, maybe I just wanted to show off my talent," he says, walking to the car and opening the door for me.

"What are you doing out this early?" I ask.

"Stocks don't wait for you to do your morning routine."

"Why don't you drive to work?" I interrogate, stepping into the car but leaving my body halfway out.

"Hey lady, can we hurry it up here?!"

I turn to see the taxi driver looking back at us. Mateo lets go of my door and knocks on the front passenger window, signaling the man to roll it down. He throws money through the window and says, "How 'bout you take the pretty lady where she needs to go and keep your mouth shut."

The taxi driver scoops up the money, holding it to the light, and nods at Mateo.

"You start tomorrow at nine a.m. Meet me in the lobby of Brooks on Wall Street." He gives me a smile while softly closing the taxi door, his hands in the pockets of his suit as he casually walks away down the street.

I meet the taxi driver's eyes in his review mirror when he says, "I need an address, ma'am."

I give the driver my address and start making a mental list of what could possibly go wrong with me working at the

Law firm. A tremble wracks my body when I realize this could actually be good for me. Maybe it's time to put my dreams aside and become an adult. Yet, in the back of my mind, I still have mixed emotions about letting go of my career dreams.

Chapter Fifteen

Jace

♫ "I Wanna Be Yours" - Artic Monkeys ♫

It's 4:30 a.m., which means Mateo is late. He is never late. He walks this route every Monday morning, leaving his house on Kingston Ave and walks to the Club Opal underground parking garage to grab his car after drinking all Sunday. Then he goes to work on Wall Street. Tuesday through Friday, he stays at his apartment in the Financial District. But today... today he is late. Something threw him off his schedule and I don't like that. I don't like that I missed what threw him off his routine.

I pull out my phone and open the paragraph I have typed and retyped a thousand times since last night. I left her in the room after she slapped me to head to the *jacks.* Partially to calm myself down and partially to stuff my dick under my belt. Then I had to roam to the back of the club since I noticed Mateo was with new people—people he has never been seen with at the club—so I stood back and listened. While they were drunkenly babbling, I was doing facial recognition on my computer at the next table over. When I came back to the room, Lily was fast asleep on the couch. I stayed all night, watching as her lips were parted, her breasts moving up and down, her eyes fluttering.

I delete the message again and decide to pull up the website I've been searching on. I noticed the way she looked at my sweater when we were in the car together. The way her eyes kept gazing at my leather jacket in the coffee shop. My *álainn* likes high fashion, so high fashion she gets.

In the corner of my eye, I spot Mateo's car pulling out the garage and heading east toward the Brooklyn Bridge. I whip my car around and head to Kingston Ave, parking across the street from his house. This is day six of no movement from either of his neighbors. My eyes dart down to my buzzing phone in the cupholder, and I press the green button when I see the caller ID.

"I think his neighbors are alias," Rowan says. "Herberta Novinski and Charles Sway. The names don't pop up in the systems. They're ghosts."

"Does this mean you're ready to come out of hiding? We need to see what Mateo is hiding in this house."

"I am not in hiding," Rowan spits.

"You're hiding," I tease. "It's been three months since we have seen John. I think he is done with us."

"Yeah, we will see about that."

He thinks John is going to come after us since Rowan's dad went missing. John warned us that he was going to kill Lance—Rowan's dad—and if he couldn't find Lance... Well, we don't know what John will do. Lance took the mafia princess, Joan, because he's a selfish fucker. Then, when the mafia was ready to come claim their prize, Lance was ready to cough up his whole family just to save his own ass. He could have picked any woman in the world, but he just had to have the biggest balls in the game. Rowan said he got a ping on Lance's location. Last he was seen was at an airport three hours after Rowan almost beat him to death.

"Do you expect me to go to jail for breaking and entering because my best friend decided to stay home and rot instead of spotting for me?" I ask.

"What makes you think I would let you have all the action while I sit in the car and watch?"

I suck on my teeth, shaking my head.

"Look, man, Celeste's art show is in a month. I'll come out of *hiding* then. I've just been trying to prepare what to say—or do—to try and explain or make up—"

I can already see Rowan sliding his hands through his hair and hanging his head. "Yeah, yeah. Save it, lover boy. I don't want to hear that shit."

I scan my key card so that the elevator can take me to my penthouse. My mind feels empty as I wait for it to stop on the twenty-fifth floor. When it finally opens, I step out into my living room and head straight to my mini bar, pouring myself a glass.

I stare at my phone as the unknown number calls for the eighth time today, taking a sip as I watch it hang up and leave a voicemail. My finger hovers over the delete button but I regrettably press play instead.

*"Ya know—*hiccup*—you can call your old man sometimes. I haven't heard from—*hiccup*—you in over a year. How do you think that makes me feel? I am—*hiccup*— all alone in this house and I sit here thinking..."*

The line is silent for a moment.

"You know what? Fuccck you, Jace. I raised you."

I scoff, shaking my head as I head toward my couch with my phone still in hand.

*"You ungrateful little shit. I should have buried you with your mother when she died. All you ever did was ruin my life from the time you—*hiccup*—were born."*

My thumb lingers over the delete button, ready to erase another voicemail from my shit-faced father. It surprises me he still owns a business. Occasionally, my mind wanders and I end up in front of the store he has in Queens. His hardware store has kept his drug and alcohol addiction in the run. Some days I see him helping a customer. Other days, he's passed out the counter. Probably hungover or high.

"All I need is a couple of dollars. Something to get me through—"

And there it is. His only request from his only son. Money. The only time my father calls me multiple times a day is when he needs money. As a kid, I looked up to him. He was a business owner of a great shop, a loving father and husband. He used to take me to his store, teach me all the tools and how to properly use them. He taught me life skills, how to read people—learn what they want and use it to your advantage. Change their motive for your benefit. For the first couple of years, my mom and I were proud of his store. It was popular since Queens didn't have a hardware store at the time. He was bringing in cash like he had won the lottery every night.

Until cancer took my mother away.

It wasn't sudden. We knew she was sick. We had hope, though. The doctor had told us we'd caught it early and she would receive the treatment she needed. All was well. Until it wasn't. One morning, she didn't wake up. That morning, our life turned upside down and was washed with darkness.

I learned to cope, my father didn't. He had no other vice but me. Everything reminded him of her, me included. From my blonde hair to my pale blue eyes, my accent, my mannerisms... Everything was a reminder of her to him.

Which led to frustration and anger.

Abuse.

When I met Rowan and Joan, I stopped going home. It was easy to run from the dark. Me not being home led to my father using and drinking himself *almost* to death. One day, when I'd had enough of his drunken episodes, he showed up unannounced at Rowan's house, screaming my name from their front lawn. I knew Rowan had his own struggles within his household and I wasn't going to be that extra tally for him. So, when I was fourteen, I emancipated myself. I stopped showing up for school and started working for different criminal organizations, going by the name Jace Cook. When Rowan's father wasn't home, I would stop by his house since he was my only true friend. Then, when we turned eighteen, he moved in with me, and that is when we started DWYM. Which was a long process. We finally got everything up and running the same year Joan went missing.

My finger finally presses the delete button, and I fling my phone next to me on the couch, taking another sip of my drink. Goosebumps develop on my skin at the thought of seeing my father in person after all these years. Have his eyes turned murky yellow? Does his skin have splotches and craters? Has his hair turned from inky black to faded grey?

I close my eyes, inhaling the ice-cold air, and imagine the one thing in my life that has not turned to absolute shit. Lily. I still remember the first time I ever saw her.

Three years ago

We are in Axel's office, trying to come up with a contract deal. Rowan and Axel keep bumping heads like some damn mountain goats because neither of them like each other's offers. So now they are staring each other to see who will crack first.

"Ye know, if you lads want to have a dick measuring contest, I can go find a ruler," I say, holding in a laugh and smiling wide at them.

Rowan's neck cracks toward me, his eyes blazing with fire. He hates when I deepen my accent, and I find it feckin' hilarious. The older he gets, the easier it is to irritate him.

"One section, a bottle a night, and thirty percent of the contracts," Axel says.

Rowan laughs, shaking his head. "You're out of your fucking mind. Thirty percent?!"

"Most of your business is going to come from my dim-wit customers, anyway," Axel snaps.

Rowan leans on Axel's desk. "A VIP room, unlimited alcohol, and three percent of contracts."

Axel stares at him, the room quiet while I sit back and watch them both fume in annoyance.

Axel crosses his arms across his chest. "One mid-section in the back of the club, unlimited alcohol, and fifteen percent."

Rowan stands from his chair, pushing it back on the floor. "Come on, Jace. We are leaving."

I shake my head. "Rowan, we need this," I whisper.

Rowan's eyes roll back before he turns toward Axel and states, "A VIP room, unlimited alcohol, and ten percent of the fucking contracts!" He points his fingers at Axel.

"Deal," Axel states calmly, holding out his hand to shake. Rowan takes his hand and is yanked closer to Axel's face. Axel's eyes enlarge and he whispers, "I would have done it for three percent."

"You fucking—"

"Alrighty! We start tonight. Thank you for the business, Axel. Let us know when you hear of someone in need." I grab Rowan, pulling him toward the door and out of this office before he ends up blowing this whole place to smithereens.

We are met at Axel's door by Roxxie, his assistant. "Follow me," she says.

We head downstairs toward the main floor. My head rolls in circles as I take in the club. When I first met Axel years ago, he told me about his vision for this club and it feels surreal seeing it come to life. My body is jolted back and I come to a stop. I look down at a head full of blonde hair. She looks up at me with glimmering green eyes. My jaw clenches as her cheeks turn a perfect strawberry color to match her strawberry perfume.

"Oh. I'm so sorry," she whispers, her fingers darting to the hem of her shirt, rubbing on it.

I've never been so tongue-tied in my life. I know I am standing here like a feckin' *eejit* unable to move out of her way. The longer I stand here staring down at her, the brighter her cheeks get. What feels like an eternity of being lost in her eyes only lasts a couple of seconds. She side-steps me and goes around, leaving me stunned. Rowan shakes his head at me before he continues to follow Axel's assistant.

I turn around to take another look at her. Her head on a swivel the same time as mine and our eyes connect. She will be the *chuisle mo chroí.*

Chapter Sixteen

Jace

♫ "Twist" - Korn ♫

I was able to find a warehouse right outside of Cold Springs. The warehouse is small, industrially constructed on the inside and broken down and abandoned on the outside. Which is perfect for my activities. I haven't had time to add the lockers and shelves to hide the toys, so I'm forced to make do with what I have handy and with what I keep in the trunk of my car. I also forgot to buy a generator, which means there is no electricity inside, no heater, no lights, plus the constant downpour in Cold Springs has created a leak in the roof. It's the perfect nightmare.

I open the door, hearing water droplets clink into a puddle, followed by mumbling in a far corner. "Guess what I found?" I say into the dark, increasing my accent. I walk toward the last location I remember putting him. It's been a couple of days since I dropped him off. I decided to let him think about his actions before I started forcing consequences. "An LED cordless lamp!"

My foot hits the body. "Oh shit. Sorry lad." I turn on the lamp to see James hogtied on the floor near my feet. James, the lovely co-worker of Mateo, was kind enough to spill too much information at Club Opal while Mateo was too busy scanning the crowd for my *álainn*. He brought up something about Italy, girls, and his new wife who also *disappeared.* Lucky for him, it was his first wife. No warning signs were raised when he filed a missing person report in New York. But it did raise a big red flag for me, and lucky for me, my favorite color is red.

"Let's get ye off this floor, yeah?" I shine the lamp throughout the warehouse, spotting a folded metal chair in the corner. "Oh, perfect." I grab it, dragging the legs of the chair to screech against the concrete. I plop it right next to James, pulling down the metal seat and sitting. I shine the lamp on the busted lad, who is currently lying in his own piss and shit.

"Don't act scared now." My upper lip curls in disgust. "This is your fault. Ye want to be a big boy in that business, ye get big boy consequences." I lift his arm and place him into the seat. I'd decided to duct tape his whole face when I abducted him, only leaving room around his nose to breathe— which is currently leaking snot everywhere. I sigh, looking at his piss-stained suit pants, his white dress shirt spotted with crimson and dirt, all the way down to his broken toes, wondering when he lost his shoes.

"Don't leave, yeah? I'm going to go get the rest of the supplies." I set the lamp down near him, walking away, laughing. You will need to have a good amount of adrenaline and strength to want to walk around blind with all your toes broken and on the verge of frostbite.

I pull my black hoodie over my head when I exit the warehouse. The only noise around me is the rain drumming against the building and the rustle of the trees. If we don't fix our roof soon, we will have a full-on lake inside. I walk to my car, opening the truck, and bring out my bag of supplies and the rolling tray.

"Man, I just love the smell of rain," I say when I enter the warehouse again. "Ye think I should leave the door open? Air out the stench you're leaving in here?" I ask as I stand near the door, waiting. We are miles from town, miles from the nearest main road. Nobody will hear him, or me. "Nah, ye know what? I have a mask in here." I hang my bag in the air as if James could see.

I set the bag at his feet, unzipping it and pulling out the surgical scalpel, the set of pliers, more duct tape, rubbing alcohol— "Oh, would you look at that! I found some rifle bullets. They must have fallen out of the box," I tell him, turning to see him squirm in the seat. "Do you have something to say?" I ask, grabbing the scalpel. "Wait a second, lad! I'm getting a little ahead of myself. It's been a while since I have done this, it gets me all worked up." I shake my limbs, feeling my blood tingle my nerves. I grab the plastic drop cloth out of my duffle bag, spreading it out over the floor. "I hate a messy cleanup, ye know?" Walking back toward him, I push his body off the seat, watching him fall onto the floor on his left shoulder, landing in a grunt. I pick up the chair, setting it directly in the middle of the cloth, then I grab his arm to walk him toward it—or more like drag him. His feet slide across the concrete floor, making his skin get caught within the divots and debris of broken glass and nails. I can hear him whine every time I pull harder when he gets stuck, and when I look over my shoulder, all I can see is the blood trail behind us.

I sit him down on the chair in front of me, dragging my rolling table and setting all my tools on top. I kneel in front of him with my scalpel in hand. "Let's get this tape off of you." I press my finger on his face where I would assume his lips would or should be. When I think I find the location, I press the blade into the tape and slash it open. His cry immediately erupts as crimson starts leaking from the opening

I just made. "Whoops, caught a little skin, didn't I?" I grab the opening of the tape and start to unravel it like a mummy, taking some of his eyebrow hairs, mustache, and a little bit the hair on his head. Throwing the tape to the side, I see I cut the corner of his lip into his cheek.

"P-please!" he cries.

"*Please, oh please!*" I mock. "Ye think your missing wife is saying the same thing right now? Begging for her life? Begging for a savior?" I hiss, turning and walking away. "I know you're going to get me heated, so I might as well open the door. Let that cool air in. I don't like overheating while I'm working." I slam the door open, taking a deep inhale, and watch as the trees dance in the distance.

I stand there until I see the sky glow white. I count in my head: *one Mississippi, two Mississippi…* I make it all the way to ten and stop when the earth rumbles. The lightning struck two miles away, which means I have to make this quick before I am electrocuted in this metal warehouse. This weather and town forces me realize how much I'm accustomed to living in the city. Hearing nature sounds rather than traffic and construction is like angels whispering into my ears. I think I should start getting out of the concrete jungle more often. Maybe take Lily somewhere nice up north? I take a palm sized rock and place it near the door frame to keep it open.

When I turn around, James is sobbing with his head down. "I can make this real simple for you, only a couple of questions," I say, walking toward him. "I need locations and names."

"I don't know, man. I swear!"

"Ye don't know?" I pick up the pliers. "Ye don't know where they sent your wife?"

"No! No! I don't!" His eyes bug at the tool in my hand.

I snap, losing control, losing my accent, losing any humanity. I shove my fist into his busted mouth and pull his jaw down. I take the pliers and grip at his front tooth, securing the pliers in place, I start to tug. "Where is your wife, James?!"

He gargles as his snot and spit collects in the back of his throat.

"WHERE ARE THE WOMEN, JAMES?!"

I pull down, his tooth snapping out easily... "It's fake?" I shove my fist into his mouth again to see his shaven down-tooth. Fucking veneers. "Typical." I spit.

I walk around him and pull his tied-up hands through the opening of the chair. I grip the scalpel and rubbing alcohol and set them down next to me.

"Who's involved, James? Who gives you orders?" I take the scalpel, wedging it under his short fingernail bed and lift up slightly to give myself a better grip with the pliers.

"Please! I don't know who!"

"Oh, but I think you do!" I end my sentence with his fingernail tucked between my pliers, and I rip it right off. The raw, irritated skin barely leaks any blood due to his wrists being bound so tightly. I take the rubbing alcohol and pour it over his open skin.

He screams out, begging for mercy, begging for God. God can't save him, no one can. Not from me. Not when I feel the heat soaring in my blood, not when I love seeing red against the white plastic cover on the floor. Not when his begs and cries sound like lullabies' in my ears. His mercy is that I will kill him—that's the type of mercy he will get. Either when I'm finished playing or when he gives me answers. At the end of the day, he will die. I just hope that wherever they took his wife, she will have a less painful ending than him.

His screams go silent. When I get up and walk in front of him, I see that he's passed out. I grab him by the back of his neck, sitting him up straight and slamming my fist into his abdomen. "Stay with me, James," I grit between my teeth.

He throws up all over his slacks and I back away to avoid getting splashed. "I bet your hungry after all that." I grab the bullets I found in the bottom of my bag, "You know, when I was little, my mother used to make me soup when I was sick. It was this delicious potato and leek soup." I rub the icy metal between my fingers. "She used to tell me that eating made you feel better." I grab his jaw, squeezing. "Don't you want to *feel* better, James?" I place my index finger into his mouth, pulling his jaw down. "Aren't you *hungry*, James?"

When his jaw is open enough, I push the bullet inside. "Swallow it," I demand. The 7mm Rem Mag is not going to go down easy. And if I were to keep him alive, it wouldn't come out easy either. I grab the rubbing alcohol. "Need something to drink with it?" I pour it down his throat, tipping his head back. "Swallow it!" I scream.

And he does. He does swallow the bullet. A little smile tips my lips. "What a good boy, James." I slap his cheek in appraisal.

I walk behind him, ready to go at his fingernails again. I kneel on the floor, grabbing the pliers. I doubt I will get answers from him, but if I have to take every man down one by one—

I close my eyes, my face sprayed with hot liquid and my ears ringing with a piercing echo. I drop the pliers and rub my hands down my face, grinning wide when I see them covered in red.

I then realize that the piercing echo was a gunshot, but there shouldn't be anyone here but me. I stand up, seeing Rowan standing in the doorway with his gun in the air. I look down at James, his neck broken back over the chair, looking up at me with clear, lifeless eyes and a bullet hole lodge in the middle of his forehead.

"Goddammit, Rowan!" I yell.

"He won't give you any answers," he states as his loafers clink against the concrete.

"Well, I won't ever know that for sure now, will I?" I point to James as his eyeballs slowly start to roll to the back of his head.

Rowan stares at me as if I'm speaking another language, his lashes blinking slowly. I huff, throwing the pliers on my tray. "It's good to see you."

"We have more work to do." He turns around, heading back to the door.

"It's good to see you too, Jace! I'm sorry I was gone for so long! I'm excited to get back to work! What have I missed?!" I holler at him while he heads to the exit. "Fucker," I whisper when the door slams.

152

Chapter Seventeen
Lily

♫ "Breathin" - Ariana Grande ♫

My stomach rumbles and my bladder suddenly feels extra full while I wait in the lobby at 9 a.m. on the dot for my first day at the law firm. I check my phone's clock for the third time in the past two minutes.

I decided to wear the only white button-down blouse I have, paired with a black pencil skirt and three-inch heels. My hair is slicked back into a clean bun, and I kept my makeup extra light. It's the perfect "I have a big girl job" outfit.

My eyes roam around the building, seeing only men. All wearing suits, carrying briefcases, either typing or talking on their phones. On command, my fingers start to rub on the portion of my untucked blouse.

This was a mistake.

I put my head down, ready to head out the front door. I'll call a cab to take me home and far away from this place.

"Lily!"

I turn to see Mateo waving his hand in the middle of the lobby. My heart falls to the scorching coffee residue that is lingering in my stomach, my feet planted to the floor underneath me as I stare and watch him stride my way. I am closer to the exit. I can turn around and pretend I never saw him and continue to work at the club.

"Sorry I'm late. This morning has been hectic. Let me show you to your floor."

Mateo is wearing a cashmere two-piece suit. His hair is parted down the middle, yet out of his face with rimless glasses barely on the tip of his nose. I lick at my dry lips, feeling as if I am being swallowed whole. My heart pounds in my chest and I'm sweating from every pore in my body.

"Hey. Hey!" His arms reach out, grabbing onto my shoulders. "Look, I know it looks crazy right now, but I promise you, your floor is more... calm. I know you're worried, but you're going to do great." He gives me a small smile, his thumb rubbing along my collar bone. His tone makes my heart beat a little less fast. I take a large breath and lift my shoulders back and chin up.

The elevators open to the fourth floor. White cubicles surround every square inch, with greyish blue carpets and whitewashed walls. Mateo's hand wraps around my bicep as he leads me to an empty cubicle that only has one computer, one notepad, and one pen.

"This one is yours. I know it looks—"

"Like stale bread," I interrupt. The only thing that is missing is the poster of a cat hanging onto a tree branch that says, *Hang in there.*

Mateo's shoulders bob up and down with laughter. "I will be right here at twelve o'clock to meet you for lunch."

I turn around to face him, his cinnamon eyes shining as he stares at me. I give him a nod and set my purse down on my L shaped desk and pull my chair out. When I turn back to him, he is already gone.

I don't even know what I am doing, what am I supposed to be working on? When I open the computer, a loud bang hits my desk, papers scattering everywhere.

"Hey."

I swivel my chair around to see a woman maybe around my age, standing behind me. Her curly hair is in a top bun, and she is wearing sweats, a large T-shirt, and slip-on shoes.

"We need these done by the end of the week," she says.

"I'm sorry—" I look back to the paperwork, my eyebrows scrunched together. "I'm new here, I wasn't really told much—" I close my mouth when she lets out a loud annoyed sigh and rubs at her eyes.

"I know you're new. It's easy. You just have to add all the numbers into the charts. That's it." She waves her hands in the air and walks away.

I keep blinking, trying to moisten my dry eyes. I can feel the carpel tunnel already settling within my bones. I've barely made a dent in the stack of papers. She wasn't wrong, it is easy, but she could have mentioned this laptop is as old as dinosaurs. It's worse than mine at home.

By the time I look at the clock, three hours have passed. I peek my head from above my cubical at the sound of the elevator ding to see Mateo walking toward me. He is speaking on the phone and the closer he gets, the angrier he sounds. His eyebrows are pinched, and his hand is balled into a fist. When he stands in front of me, he hangs up the phone.

"You ready?" he asks, his frown contouring into a smile. I pick up my bag and follow him back into the elevator and down to the lobby.

We make it through the crowd to a bar down the street.

"So how do you like it so far?" Mateo questions as he takes a sip of his beer.

"It was—" I have no words. I don't even think I have a thought in my brain. All the numbers I have read are imprinted into my head. My brain cells went from five to one. I'm nervous to pick up my drink because my fingers are so sore.

Mateo reaches for my hand, settling his on top of mine. When I look at him, his lips are pinched into a small smile. "Look, I know it probably isn't the best. But the pay is great and it's quiet." He removes his hand and sits back. "I'm probably being selfish," he says while shaking his head. "I'm just trying to persuade you to stay there so I can see you more often."

My eyes widen at his confession.

"It's true though. I would like to see you more often, Lily. If that's okay? You don't have to stay at the firm, but I would still like to see you more often. Maybe a date? Not just for coffee and lunch breaks."

I bite at my bottom lip, feeling my cheeks burst into flames. I've been seeing Mateo for years at the club. Have always denied him a chance with me. I never had a good reason besides the fact that he is my customer at work. "Mateo—"

"Are you guys ready to order?" the waitress interrupts, standing by our table with her notepad.

PART TWO

Chapter Eighteen

Lily

One Month Later…

♫ "No Good" - Roux ♫

I stare at the box on my bed that displays the very famous French luxury brand. It was delivered anonymously last week. The only person who I assume would send me these nude pump heels would be Mateo.

Or Jace.

I decided to give Mateo a chance and ignore Jace's threat. Mateo is harmless, he is like a little mouse begging for cheese. So, I am going to assume that these heels are from Mateo and move on with my life and any thoughts of Jace. I haven't been back to the club to see Jace since I started working at the firm. Sitting there at the computer from nine to five, working on matter numbers, has been more exhausting than I expected. At least I've started summer break at school, so my sleep schedule is slowly going back to normal.

"Come on, Lily. We are going to be late!"

I flip the top of the box open and quickly put on the shoes and run my hands down the dress I made. Short, tight, and accentuating my curves in all the right places—and yes, I did add the *Cruella de Vil* look.

"Is that Louis Vuitton?!" Celeste bends down to get a closer look. I take a step back, the hair on my neck feeling sticky. "Was I sleeping or something?! When did you get these?" she asks.

"Um... From a friend. Now come on we are going to be late. It's your big day!" I grab her hand, pulling her out of the house.

Last-minute details are being added around the place—balloons, drinks, there is even a DJ in the corner. I introduce myself to Alicia, thanking her for recognizing how wonderful my best friend is and for giving her a show.

When the doors open, all my law school classmates pile in, including Mateo. He does a quick look around before finally spotting me. Butterflies pile in my stomach when he smiles and looks down at the floor as if he is the nervous one.

He grabs my hand, kissing me on the cheek. "You look fantastic. And so does this place."

Mateo's dark fluffy hair has grown out. His black and white suit, tie, and loafers make me want to melt right here. We both grab a champagne glass from a waiter walking around. The place immediately starts bursting with laughter and conversation. I watch Celeste go around speaking to all the guests, thanking them for coming. I introduce Mateo to some of my classmates and of course, he tries to persuade them to come work at the law firm in his building.

Mateo excuses himself to find a bathroom, giving me the opportunity to finally look around at Celeste's paintings. I start heading toward her biggest one, *The Bell Jar*, but before I make it there, I notice a tall man with dark wavy hair walking up behind her. I can't see his face since his back is toward me, but it's like he is almost sneaking up on her. I start walking faster, ready to go see who the hell thinks they can sneak up on a woman like that, but a gasp leaves my lips when my arm is pulled backward. My drink spills from its glass as my body is whiplashed into darkness.

"What the fuck?!" I hold my hands out to try and feel for something since I can't see anything, but I stop moving when my hand hits a body. "Um, hello? Mateo, this is not funny. Find a light."

I hear a soft click to my right, and I squeeze my eyes to adjust to the brightness. When my vision clears, I find myself face to face with Jace. He looks like he did the first day I saw him on my doorstep when Celeste and Rowan went to Italy. His hair is longer, covering most of his forehead and curling up on the ends. His under eyes are smeared purple and his stubble has grown out, taken shape to accentuate his jaw. He's wearing a suit and tie and god, he looks good. *Really good.* The room feels like its closing in on me as his mesmerizing blue eyes stare into mine. My breath hitches as the air becomes thicker around us. "Um, hi?"

His eyes leave mine, traveling down my body, stopping on my shoes before he makes his way back up. "Quit your job, Lily."

Not this again. Talk about a mood destroyer. I turn around, realizing we are in a storage closet. I set my glass down on an empty shelf before facing him again and cross my arms over my chest. "Look Jace, I don't know what your issue is, but seriously, get over it." He takes a step forward, forcing me to take a step back. "We had our fun. Our time was once and over. It was a mistake. I regret it and we should have never gone that far," I say, but the words taste like tar on my tongue.

He takes another step, only inches away from me. "You regret it?"

I lean closer to him, staring into his eyes. "My biggest regret," I snarl.

His finger lazily slides across my arm and my body decides to betray me by sending chills down my spine. "If I am your biggest regret, then why are your nipples so hard right now?" He curls his mouth upward, showing his teeth.

I swat his hand away from me. "Don't fucking touch me." I push his chest to give myself room to breathe, to think. Fuck, this is a small closet. "I will pay you back as soon as I have the full amount. But I swear, Jace, stay far away from me. And the payback will not be what you think it is. I will have the money." I point my finger at him.

His eyes narrow as he leans on the opposite wall. "I don't want your money."

"Then what do you want from me?!" I scream, throwing my hands in the air. At this point, I don't care if anyone hears me yelling in this closet. Give them a reason to open this closet door and come save me because I cannot find the will to save myself. I decided that day, at the bar, that I would give Mateo a chance. Me being here, in this closet, with Jace, is not a good idea. My body reacts to him in ways I've never experienced before. Anytime I see him, no matter how mad I am, no matter how much he annoys me, my body craves him. My body worships him.

"You," he responds.

My arms fall, along with my mouth. He keeps his composure calm as he stares right into my soul. The remaining oxygen is sucked straight out of this room, the back of my neck breaking into a sweat.

I almost scream when the door to the closet opens. Demi-god number two, a.k.a. Rowan, stands in the doorway looking at the both of us. "Out of the fucking closet before you cause a scene at my girl's big day," Rowan snaps.

Whatever trance Jace had me in withers away. I scoff and shoulder bump Rowan on the way out. *My girl*. Please, he has been MIA for the past four months and he thinks he can just walk in here, claiming Celeste again like nothing ever happened?

I find the nearest waiter, grabbing two champagne glasses. I down one while looking around to find Mateo.

"Don't you just love life?" Celeste says, grabbing my shoulders, smiling ear to ear with slight tears in her eyes.

"Yup," I sneer while drowning the other glass of champagne. I guess Rowan *can* just walk in here and claim Celeste like nothing happened.

Rowan comes up behind her and kisses her on the top of her head. I roll my eyes, turning the other way to see Jace coming out the closet and heading out the front door. In the distance, I can see Mateo finally make his appearance. He looks at Jace, then at me, his scowl wiped off and replaced with a grin.

Mateo walks to my side. "Mr. Harper, how you doing?" He holds out his hand, but Rowan takes a moment before grabbing it. I can't tell if Mateo sees the hesitation, but it is obvious to me. When I look at Mateo, he's still grinning from ear to ear. What is the big drama between these three? Jace hates Mateo and now Rowan does too?

"Mr. Davenport, good to see you," Rowan says.

I grab two more champagne glasses from a waiter passing by. I'm not taking my time enjoying the acidic bubbly taste. All three people standing in front of me watch as I finish a glass in one gulp. For some reason, I can't stop and don't want to stop. I feel like I'm drowning, and I can't tell if it's because I'm physically drowning myself with these drinks or because, for the first time in over a month, I saw Jace. He shouldn't make me feel this way. I don't know why he makes me feel this way.

"Looks like I have to take this one home," Mateo says, laughing with my friends.

At least he *thought* Celeste and Rowan were going to laugh. Instead, Rowan is staring at me with a blank face and Celeste's eyebrows are pinched together.

"I'm fine," I reply sharply. I immediately feel bad for the tone, but that feeling is soon gone when his hand grabs my bicep with force. I lower the glass from my lips and eye him. I try to remove my arm from him, but he tightens his fingers even harder.

I turn toward Celeste, my head leaning slightly to the side, thinning my lips in a tight smile. "Celeste, babe, I am so proud of you. I will see you at home, m'kay?"

Celeste nods her head in understanding and leans her head back to look up at Rowan. Mateo releases my arm, allowing me to give her a hug before I stomp toward the door.

I stand at the sidewalk, waiting for a cab. When Mateo reaches my side, I turn toward him. "Don't ever touch me like that again."

He turns to me, tipping his chin down to look at me over his glasses. "I'm sorry?"

"What you did back there was not okay. If I want to drink, I will drink. I am a big girl and can handle myself. But you holding my arm like that—like I'm a pet, your pet"—I point my red fingernails right in his face— "will never happen again. You touch me with respect. You touch me like I'm fucking treasure. A pile of gold. Or you don't touch me at all."

His eyes turn into large circles as his mouth gapes open. I don't know how he treated his past wives, but I am not them. I recollect all the times Jace has gripped me. The day he was at my house, he pulled my arm back and whipped me into his chest and told me not to fake an accent. When he grabbed my arm and told me not to run away from him at the club, dragging me to the front door. Tonight, when he pulled me in the closet. Yet, none of it compares to how Mateo just grabbed me. Jace's force somehow feels soft and careful. Mateo's grip could leave bruises.

"I'm sorry, baby. I didn't mean it like that. I didn't mean to hurt you." He steals my hand, kissing all my fingers.

I don't show my forgiveness. Instead, I open the door to the cab that just pulled to the curb, get in, and close the door behind me.

Chapter Nineteen

Jace

♫ "Save the World" - We Are Not Friends & Nextime ♫

That was not how I wanted it to go. I didn't mean to confess to Lily but seeing her there, wearing the shoes I bought her... I shake my head as I continue racing down to Rowan's house.

In a feckin' closet, Jace?

Rowan told me he was going to be awhile and stay at the art exhibit with Celeste, but asked me to meet him at his house. We both didn't expect Mateo to be there. I especially didn't anticipate seeing him there with Lily. Something just took over me. I needed her. I needed her to be alone. Seeing her in the shoes sent fire through my blood. I would have allowed her to step on my neck with those shoes if she wished. She will keep receiving gifts just so that I can feel like I am a part of her.

I drive through Rowan's gate, park my car, and walk up the stairs to his white two-story home that looks like it should be in the country—not a couple of miles from the city. I knock on his door, waiting for Rowan's new bodyguard, Noah to answer. Noah was a part of the deal we made with Axel. The deal was, in order for us to investigate Mateo, we had to hire Noah. Noah is new to the business and is obligated to go through a performance check before Axel puts him up for hire. The only issue is, Rowan had to put his pride aside and allow Noah to stay at his house. Rowan doesn't allow anyone to know where he lives. With him being New York City's number one bachelor multi-billionaire drama queen— he'd rather not have anyone sneaking around his property trying to catch his next scandal. Except Celeste. Only a few months ago, we saw her trying to sneak into Club Opal. She waited hours for us to leave the club and followed Rowan all the way home. Rowan claims he allowed her to follow, but I say otherwise.

I'm a fan of Noah. He talks to us and loves to state his opinion on things whether he is asked or not. It pisses Rowan off, which makes me like him even more. He is younger than us, but just as tall and built. He will be able to handle his shit if he stays on this career path.

"Hey, man." Noah swings his body to the side, letting me in.

I walk past him and head straight for the kitchen's highest shelf, finding exactly what I need.

Whiskey.

I pour a double shot, taking it within seconds, then pour another.

"Party was that good, huh?" Noah comments, sitting at the kitchen island.

"Was a blast. You should have been there." I close my eyes, shaking my head, and feel the burn on my tongue down my throat.

The front door opens as Rowan comes striding in, removing his coat and opening his computer.

"What happened?" I ask, sitting on the chair next to him in the living room.

"We have to plan this very carefully," he states, banging his fingers on the keyboard.

I can feel my body temperature rising, either from the alcohol or from the fact that Rowan isn't stating what the fuck happened. We sit in silence while Rowan continues to work on his computer.

"So much communication here. I love it," Noah says, releasing his sarcasm for the day.

Rowan finally snaps out of his trance and looks up at us. He runs his hands through his hair and lets out a deep breath.

"We need to find Ana. Dead or alive. But I have this deep feeling that she is not alive." Rowan sits back on the couch, staring at his computer.

"You think Mateo killed her?" I ask. I can feel my fist clenching and unclenching at the thought of a man who murdered his wife being near Lily.

"Possibly, yeah."

"If he killed her, then why hire us to find her?" I question.

Rowan turns toward me and Noah. "That is what I am worried about."

It doesn't matter what time of the day it is. We will always find Axel at the club. All three of us follow Roxxie up the stairs to his office. She knocks on the door before opening it and letting us in. Axel, being the weird mysterious man he is, turns around in his oversized throne to face us. "Well, if it isn't the three stooges."

"Hey man, don't include me in yet. I just started," Noah drawls as he goes to lean back against a wall. Rowan and I take the seats in front of Axel's desk.

"What can I do for you guys?"

I turn my head toward Rowan since I am not sure what we are even doing here. We already made the deal to investigate Mateo, so how much more would Axel be willing to give us?

"Why did Mateo hire protection?" Rowan casually asks as he gets more comfortable in the chair.

Axel leans back, staring at both of us. Yes, Rowan and I might be taller than average, but Axel... This man towers over us by at least three inches. With his miscolored eyes and youthful look, he could be *Aengus Óg*.

"Now, you know that is client confidentiality," Axel states.

"We agreed that if we take him on"—Rowan points back toward Noah— "that you will allow us to investigate Mateo. This is us investigating."

"Well, go investigate somewhere else," Axel snaps.

There is a quiet breeze from the AC, the tension in the room thick as mud. When I open my mouth to clear the air, Noah beats me to it.

"Well, this is awkward. Looks like we are done here."

Only Noah has the balls to speak whatever is in his head no matter who he is around. I stand from my chair, ready to leave. When I look at Rowan, his eyes are shooting daggers at Axel. Axel stares back, tapping his finger on his chair. They might as well pull their dicks out and have a sword fighting contest.

Finally, Rowan stands, nodding his head at Axel before we all walk out of his office.

"What was the point of that?" I ask.

"To see Mateo's protection level." Rowan pulls his keys out to unlock his car when we enter the parking garage.

"I don't get it," Noah states.

For me, a lightbulb clicks on. The "client confidentiality" is bullshit. Axel has told us about the men he protects without hesitation, but it is usually the lower-level men—the men who are just scared they will be attacked for owing some sharks money. Men worried about the media finding their gambling and sex addictions. If Axel can't tell us why Mateo needs protection, then this is something bigger than we expected, with the added possibility that Axel wants Mateo taken out, since he is allowing us to investigate in the first place.

I nod my head at Rowan in understating before getting in my car.

Noah is standing in the middle of the street looking between us. "Hold on, I still don't get it. What am I missing?"

Chapter Twenty

Lily

♫ "Favorite Part" - Sabrina Claudio ♫

I spin around in my chair, waiting for the green screen and random codes to stop lining my computer. My spinning stops when my phone starts to ring, and I look at the caller ID before quickly answering.

"Hi, Ma."

The line is silent for a moment. "Baby, can you hear me?" my mom asks.

"Yes, Mom, can you hear me?" I lean my head back over my chair and continue to make myself nauseated by orbiting in a circle.

"How's work? How is college going? You're on speaker, Papa is sitting next to me."

I can hear my brothers and sisters in the background, running around while my mother tries to speak over them. Sometimes I miss a loud house. Our house has been extra quiet since Celeste stays at Rowan's more often and the silence creeps me out. I'm starting to hear every noise in the wall.

"Everything is great." I mask a happy voice, when in reality, I hate it. I hate the cubicles. I hate the growing, eerie silence every day, only hearing other people fingering their computers while I try to work on numbers, day after day. But for some sickening reason, I can't find it in myself to leave, to disappoint Mateo, to disappoint my mother and father. They are finally seeing their firstborn live out a dream. *Their dream.*

"That's fantastic, Lily."

"And you're staying away from those boys, correct?" my father interrupts.

My mother responds in our native language, cursing him out by telling him I am old enough. I also catch her whispering that I need to find a husband, but I am going to pretend I didn't hear it.

My computer screen finally stops acting like this is the *Matrix* and returns to the fashion website. Summer is the only time I have when I can really focus on fashion. I set my phone down, putting it on speaker while my mother continues talking to my father and my little sister screams at my brother about a toy.

This is what my family check-ups tend to consist of: a constant screaming phone conversation between my family in Athens and me, in New York, listening.

Over the yelling of my mother and siblings, I hear my doorbell ring. I tell my parents I have to go and that I love them, hanging up before they can give me a response.

I quickly answer the door to find a delivery man with a large rectangular box in hand.

"Miss Ballis?"

"Yes?"

He passes me his phone to sign off my name and throws the box into my hands. I close the door, running to the living room, and throw the black velvet box on the couch. There are no labels, and no stickers stating who sent this to me.

I remove the top box to see a black one-shoulder draped maxi dress. My mouth drops to the floor. A designer dress—one that I have had my eyes on for weeks, that is tabbed about twelve times in my search history. I pick up the card that fell onto the floor when I removed the top.

For tonight.

No name again. First it was the shoes, now the dress. I run to my room, picking up my phone. As soon as I unlock it, I get a text from Mateo.

Mateo: Picking you up at six. Be ready.

I can feel my cheeks start to burn as I stand here, smiling at my phone.

I do some final touches to my makeup—bold red lips and natural shimmer eyeshadow—and make sure all the pins in my hair are tightly secured into an updo. I add simple jewelry, making sure nothing is bold enough to take away from the dress.

On cue—six on the dot—my doorbell rings. I put on my black heels with a touch of red and grab my purse. I open the door to find Mateo standing outside in a black and white tux. His hair is combed and gelled back and he's wearing his glasses that I find so adorable.

He holds out his hand to walk me to the car.

"Thank you, by the way," I say while rubbing my hands along the dress.

He holds the door open while peering at me. "You don't have to thank me yet. I haven't told you where we are going." He laughs while closing the door. I follow his movement as he rounds the car to the driver's side.

"Yeah, but the dress is beautiful. You didn't have to do that," I say when he enters the car.

He turns to me, lips curving only slightly as he looks at me from head to toe. "Do what? The dress *is* nice though, you look good."

I trap the air in my lungs, pressing my tongue to the roof of my mouth. I give him a small smile and nod before glancing to face the front window. If Mateo didn't send the dress, then that only means one other person... The fabric feels too tight along my skin, and I suddenly want to rip the dress off.

The drive to our location is silent and awkward. Afterwards, Mateo trails around the car to open my door and hands his keys to VIP. His hand lingers against my waist as he drags me inside.

"An opera?" I take my seat next to him, but he doesn't respond. Instead, he stands when someone tries to pass us to get to their seats.

"Mr. Wheeler, nice to see you," he says, shaking the hand of some older man in a suit.

This is a business outing. Not a date. How naive of me to think this was about us. The old man turns to look at me, undressing me with his eyes as his wife stands next to him, while he continues to shake Mateo's hand. Mateo notices, looking at me and back to the older man.

"Mr. Wheeler, this is Lily, my—"

My head swivels to Mateo, my heart dropping out my ass. His what? We've never talked about this. Hell, he still hasn't taken me on an official date.

"This is Lily," he finishes.

I stand, grabbing Mister Old-fucking-pervert's hand and shaking it. His smile widens when he uses both of his hands to grab mine. "Very nice to meet you, Lily."

I take my seat again, wiping my *now* slimy hands along my dress. Mateo sits, turning to face Mr. Wheeler, just yapping away with him before the show starts. I tap Mateo on the shoulder and tell him I'm going to grab a drink since I thankfully noticed a bar by the main entrance before we walked in here.

I wait for the bartender to finish his rounds, leaning over to look at all my options. I jump in place when I feel two hands wrap around my waist, pinning me to my spot. A spicy scent invades the air around me.

"I love seeing your body wrapped in my gifts," a voice blows into my ear.

I flip around to see Jace standing right behind me. "What the fuck is wrong with you?!" I quietly squeal, looking around to see the crowd surrounding us. My eyes dart to a bathroom sign, grabbing his hand, I pull him toward it. I try to scan the crowd to see if I can spot Mateo standing anywhere, afraid of getting caught.

When we enter the bathroom, I throw him in and lock the door behind us. Jace's eyes are the color of a stormy night. He's wearing a suit with no tie, the top two buttons of his dress shirt undone, and his hair is draped across his forehead— messy, disheveled, and sexy. He's shaved off his stubble, showing off his crisp jaw. He's smiling at me like he caught my hand in the cookie jar, and it makes my heart pound against my sternum while his eyes linger up and down my body.

"You were the shoes too?" I ask, staying close enough to the door just in case I need to make a quick exit.

His tongue darts out, licking his bottom lip. He takes a step closer to me when I take a step back, putting my hand on the door handle.

"Is there an issue?" He steps even closer. My hand is still on the handle, but I am unable to turn and leave.

"Yes, there is an issue. I don't need these things. I didn't need your money to pay off school and I don't need your gifts." My breath becomes thicker as if the air is being sucked away from my lungs the closer he gets.

He bends down slightly so that his forehead rests on top of my head. I can hear him take a deep inhale before he says, "I know you don't need me, *álainn*, but I need you."

I close my eyes for a second before I snap out of it and push him away. "Jace I— I can't." I close my eyes again, shaking my head to force myself not to look at him. His outfit hugs his body, showing every indent, curve, and bulge of his muscles.

His scent.

His accent.

His everything.

"Why are you doing this?" I breathe out.

I didn't notice him step away from me, his jaw clenching before he says, "I told you to stay away from him. You're not listening." He takes off his suit jacket, throwing it into the sink to the right of him, and rolls up his dress shirt to his forearms, sliding his hands into his trouser pockets. The action is so flawless and effortless.

"So, for me not listening, you send me gifts?"

He takes one large step, pushing me back against the door. His hand glides up my thigh, bunching my dress up. His bitter cold hand rubs against my skin and my eyes roll back in memory of the one night not so long ago—his hands all over me, his mouth touching my skin...

"No. You not listening will result in consequences. The gifts"—his bottom lip rubs against my cheek to my ear— "are for my benefit." One hand grips my waist, and the other hand finds the nape of my neck, pulling my body away from the door and closer to his. I can feel my body mold and melt into his as his nose rubs against my neck. A moan escapes my mouth, my words in a chokehold. Jace's touch is electrifying, hitting every nerve. I feel like a moth dragged to a flame. My body craves the fire through his fingers. Through his soft lips against my skin. I'm in a trance I can't escape from. A cloud I cannot fall from. A dream I cannot wake from.

His finger finds my center, moving my panties to the side as he slowly swipes between my slit. "So hot and wet for me." His teeth dig into the sensitive part between my neck and shoulder.

"Jace I— I can't." I can taste the lie on my tongue. I can't find the will to make him stop. My body stands in a firepit and welcomes the heat like it's second nature.

"Don't worry." He releases my body and takes a step back, my shoulders falling as a wheeze leaves my mouth. "My time will soon come," he says, walking around me and leaving the bathroom.

I stand there, trying to catch my breath. I turn around and lock the bathroom door again. I run to the mirror to see if I look out of sorts. My face is as red as a cherry and sweat drips down my forehead. The longer I look, the more I don't recognize the person staring back at me. The woman in the mirror is a void. A replacement for what I have become. The person staring back at me is not me.

I sit silently the whole show. Mateo doesn't question why I was gone for so long. He doesn't question me for not having that drink I said I was going to go get and we make no conversation on the way home.

What am I doing? How did I end up here?

I have never been with a man longer than a few weeks, always ending it quickly for my own benefit, but for some reason, Mateo has kept me trapped. With his calm tone, never pushy about wanting sex, and with me being so busy with my new job and school—he has just been here. By my side like a ghost, and I've allowed it. I've indulged in it. And at the same time, I've never questioned it.

We pull up to my house. He turns the car off and continues to stare out the front window.

"What are we?" I ask. It's the question that haunts every man's dreams, but when he introduced me to his friend, he didn't even know how to label us. He says nothing, which says everything. "I can't do this anymore. I don't have anything at the firm so—"

"Is this because of Jace?" he asks, still looking out the window.

"I'm sorry?"

He throws his head back, laughing, his voice no longer sweet and sultry. "Is this about fucking Jace? I know you sneak around with him. I see the way you two look at each other. You can't stop being a whore for longer than a couple of weeks? Have to throw your pussy around at every guy who gives you the slightest attention? I liked you, Lily. I really did. But fuck, you're a piece of work. I even saw the way you looked at my potential business partner tonight."

He is not worth it. I open the car door and slam it so hard the window raddles. He is not worth arguing with. He doesn't know me. He doesn't know my life. I walk toward my house when a hand grabs me, whipping me around.

"I'm sorry, Lily. I didn't mean it."

I rip my arm out of his hold. "You didn't mean it? Like you didn't mean it when you were embarrassing me in front of my friends? Trying to hold me back from drinking?" A laugh rises from my throat. "And *I'm* the piece of work?"

"I'm sorry, Lily! I've just been so stressed about work and—"

I put my hand in his face. "No. Save it. I don't want excuses. I see the shiny red flag waving above your head, and I have given you more chances than you deserve." I gather my keys from my purse and walk up the steps, unlocking my door and slamming it in Mateo's face.

Chapter Twenty-One

Lily

♬ "Bad at Love" - Halsey ♬

"Okay, spill the tea."

My eyes are barely open, and I can feel the slimy morning breath lingering in my mouth. I grab ahold of my blankets, throwing them over my head. It is too early in the morning for Celeste to come wandering into my room asking questions.

"Oh, c'mon Lily." She grabs the blankets, pulling them down. "I heard you yelling last night outside the door. I saw the huge box on the couch and the expensive dress draped on the floor. I want the tea and in exchange, I bought you a coffee."

I whip my body to see Celeste sitting on my bed, holding two cups in her hands. I sit up and snatch one away from her. I take a sip, tasting a shit-ton of sugary caramel with whipped cream. I choke on it, handing it back to her, and grab the other coffee. I take a cautionary slurp and smile when I feel the warm black coffee kiss my tongue.

"Men are shit," I say, setting my coffee down on my nightstand and leaning against my headboard.

"Yes, we all know this, but what is new?" She climbs onto my bed, sitting crisscross.

"Jace is a stalker."

"Again... What is new?" Celeste hides her smile behind her coffee.

"Ugh," is the only word that I can form. What can I say? My life is corrupt. Recently, the only time my vagina works is when Jace is breathing the same air as me. Mateo must have some type of mental illness, because who the fuck decides to crash out on someone like he did to me last night and then apologize right after?

"And Mateo? I caught the look you gave me when he grabbed your arm."

Hearing his name out loud makes me want to vomit.

Actually, no.

It's not his name. It's the two empty wine bottles I see lying on the side of my bed. I remember the first bottle. The second, not so much.

"Oh, he is finished. Toasted like a strudel. And I no longer work at the firm. Back to the club I go." I jiggle my hands in the air with fake enthusiasm.

Celeste puts her drink down, laying her head next to me. "What do we want to do? Trash his house? Burn down the law firm? Crash his car?"

"Oh god." I shake my head. "You're hanging around Rowan too much." Her reaction is to laugh and pat me on top of my head, which is a little concerning.

"Well, remember when I was a sob lying in bed after Rowan and you came and told me to get my ass up?" she reminds me while rolling off the bed.

"That is because your room's stench started making its way to the whole house," I say, scrunching my nose. It took me weeks to get that smell out of my nostrils.

"Well, now it's my turn." She grabs one of my pillows, throwing it at my face. "Get your ass up, we don't sob over boys."

"Says the one running back to one!"

She gives me a nice finger gesture before heading out of my room. "Get your ass up!"

"And do what?!"

She slams my door shut without responding.

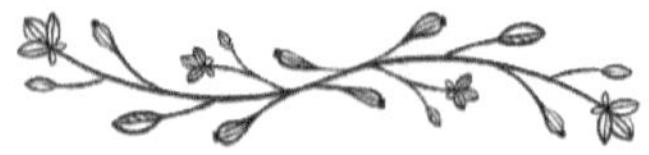

I guess Celeste yelling at me worked, because I did get my ass up. I called Marge and told her to put me on the schedule for the rest of the week. I cleaned my room, which took over four hours due to me finding random items and reminiscing over them. For example, I found an old pair of shoes I made. I don't know how I did it, but they were constructed using cut-up pieces of other shoes and random cloth. They were ugly, but I ended up trying them on and did a little dance while my playlist skimmed through all my favorite songs.

I also took a well-deserved—not needed—break and drew up another design I had in mind. Then I didn't like that design and drew another, and another. The voices in my head just kept talking and talking, telling me what to draw. I ended with a cheetah print leotard with fringe diamond bulbs at the ends.

Then I had a snack, because I couldn't remember the last time I ate. By the time I finished, I realized I had to leave for work. I took the subway and walked a couple miles before finally stepping into hell. And by hell, I mean staring at the ugly red carpet and walls of Club Opal. Marge gave me a big hug when she saw me, kissing me on the cheeks and letting me know how much she missed me. Rebecca told me to fuck off, and the other tenders... Well, they didn't care, and I don't expect them too. Except there is a new girl, Jessica, who looks way too young to be here.

After I put on my shoes, she introduces herself to me. She has long pink hair and she definitely got her boobs done. I try not to look at them while she tells me her background. The only thought in my head is asking her who her surgeon is and if I can get their number ASAP.

Marge calls out everyone's section, including mine. I smile as I get ready, finally feeling like my life is somewhat getting back to its regularly scheduled program.

When I reach my section, all the men start hollering. They ask where I have been, and I tell them that a girl has a life outside of the club. They laugh and I take a seat next to one of my regulars. He pulls money out of his wallet, shoving it into my hand, and tells me to never leave again.

A couple of hours pass by, and I get tired of listening to their work. I scan the club until my eyes stop at room five, seeing the curtain open and Jace sitting there with pink-haired bimbo Jessica. She is so close to him that her breasts could suffocate his face if she leaned any closer. Rowan is also there but not paying any attention to the sexual tension happening between those two. My eyes roam back to Jace and Jessica. He leans into her neck, whispering something to make her laugh—with her chest, not her mouth. Her breasts are like water bags, jiggling, yet her mouth stays closed.

My breathing becomes erratic. I move my hair over to one side of my shoulder, feeling the club becoming too hot. My fingers start shaking and I try to pry my eyes away, but I can't. I don't want to. They keep making googly eyes at each other and now I want to rip the new girl out of the room by her hair and mop her on this floor.

Jace looks up and spots me right away. His eyes glow in the light and he curls his lips upward, giving me a devilish grin. Jessica notices his focus is no longer on her and turns her eyes toward me. I whip my head away, bring my attention back to my clients. My ears start to ring, muffling out the voices around me. I can't find a way to calm my breathing down and when I look at my fingers, I can't force them to stop shaking. I quickly excuse myself, running to the locker room.

Jace

As soon as Lily leaves her section, I throw Jessie—Jamie? Juliet?—whatever-the-fuck-her-name-is—off me and follow her to the locker room. I open the door, finding her bent over, holding onto the benches. I slam the door behind me, scaring her. She jumps up, turning around, and I see she has tears streaming down her face and bloodshot eyes that clash against her beautiful green irises. Before I can move or even open my mouth, she marches to me, swinging her arms at my chest and screaming words I can't understand in another language.

I grab ahold of her wrists with one hand, pinning them behind her back and lifting her up by her ass. Her legs wrap around me—which I don't think she noticed—as she continues to try and wriggle out of my grip. I take us out of the locker room, making my way toward the stairs. I give Roxxie a nod before she unclicks the red rope and lets me walk up to the second floor.

"Where the fuck are you taking me?! Put me down!"

I walk us into one of the rooms, throwing her onto the couch and locking the door behind us. She turns around with wide eyes, looking around the space. I have been attending Club Opal long enough to know she has never been back here. There's a pole in the middle of the room and an all-black sectional couch that wraps around the stage. The walls are covered in windows, with a single light that highlights only the center of the floor.

I head toward the window and pull on the string to close the curtains. I watch Lily run to the door, her tall heels stopping her from running fast enough, which gives me the opportunity to reach her before she makes it out. I wrap my arm around her stomach, stopping her.

"Jace, please!" she cries.

"Just listen to me, *álainn.*" I press my face into her hair, smelling her strawberry perfume. I walk backward till I hit the couch. She falls into my lap with her back against my chest, feeling my cock twitch as her ass sits right on top of it.

"Why are we in here?" She brings her knees to her chest, curling herself into a little ball on top of me.

"Would you rather this be more public? I can open the curtains if you like," I ask while swiping her hair off her back to reveal her skin. She is wearing a tiny little shirt that cuts low down her back, paired with a tight black leather skirt. I start leaving small kisses, feeling the goosebumps rise on her skin. I can't get too ahead of myself, feeling my dick grow by the second.

I lift her off me, setting her back down while I sit on the stage in front of her. She curls back into a ball, laying her head on her knees while looking at me. I run my hands through my hair, not knowing how to tell her—ask her. This is something Rowan, Noah, and I have been planning for days. This was the only day I could ask her before time starts to run out, before it is too late.

She stares at me. Her eyebrows crinkle as she lifts her head. "Jace, are you okay?"

Am I okay? A snicker comes out of my mouth. I am about to tell the girl of my dreams to do something so fucked that I can barely comprehend it. Yet, she still finds the heart to ask *me* if I am okay. When I am about to ruin her life.

I take a deep breath, feeling like I'm about to throw up all the alcohol that is sitting in my stomach.

"Jace... you're paler than normal." She reaches her hand out, grabbing my clenched fist.

"Lily." I look up at her.

She falls back into the sofa, her eyes bulging from their sockets. "Oh god, you used my real name... What is going on?"

I smile a little, shaking my head. This is so fucked.

"Mateo is going to ask you to marry him in a couple of days and I need you to say yes."

Chapter Twenty-Two

Lily

♫ "Aphrodite" - Sam Short ♫

I stand from the couch, searching the room. I knew this whole thing with Mateo was a fucking joke. They are fucking with me. I look up at the roof, behind the pillows, under the couch.

"Lily, baby. What—What are you doing?"

I turn back around to Jace and smile so hard my cheeks start to sting. His eyes are low, pretending to look concerned. Wow, he is good. I laugh and keep looking. Jace comes to my side, grabbing my arm. "Stop, Jace." I laugh, "I'm looking for the cameras." I throw another pillow from the couch onto the ground.

"What cameras?" He takes a step back and starts to look around the room too.

"The cameras! Because you're obviously fucking with me." A laugh escapes my lips as a tear simultaneously falls down my cheek. I feel my body start to shake, my blood turning to fire, and for some reason, my hands dart out, pushing Jace back by his chest.

"*Álainn*, sit down, please. Let me explain."

I laugh again, feeling more tears pour down my face.

"Are you guys fucking insane!" I scream, standing off the couch. "Why don't you just call the fucking cops?!" Jace told me the fucked-up plan they have while he paced the room like a lunatic. I can't tell if he is nervous for asking me to do something so idiotic or if he is also worried the plan won't work. Which does not ease any thoughts I already have about it.

"I know it is crazy, but it will work." He comes to stand in front of me. His hands caress both sides of my face while his bright blue eyes stare into my soul. "I promise. I will find you."

I can feel my skin melting into his. I lean away from the couch and closer to him. We both hesitate, staring at one another as if the ground will disappear from under our feet if we move another inch. I take the initiative and crash my lips against his.

He bites at my bottom lip, forcing my mouth open as his tongue dances with mine. He pushes me back deeper into the couch. Hovering above me, he uses his knees to spread my legs apart. His hands grab the top of the couch, leaning into my face. "I promise I will find you," he repeats as he dives into my neck, sucking that sensitive spot into his mouth.

A moan escapes me as his hand grabs my breast, kneading it with his fingers. I reach for his pants, unzipping them while he flips me horizontally onto the couch. Our mouths are unable to leave each other, moving in sync as if we have kissed for a thousand lifetimes. With hunger and greed, I pull at his jeans. He removes his body from mine and shoves his jeans down just above his knees, freeing his cock.

I stare as his large hand wraps around the Jacob's ladder, squeezing once before he leans down into me, sucking my earlobe into his mouth, sending fire down my spine. His hand glides on my stomach, pulling my shirt up and over my head and pushing my skirt above my waist, bundling it up at my midriff. He takes one look at my bra and rips it in half.

"I promise to buy you a new one each time," he says, his husky voice vibrating on my skin as his mouth drops to my nipples, licking each one into his mouth. He leaves kisses down my stomach, twirling his tongue around my belly button. "I want every part of you. I want to taste every inch of your skin."

Throughout the years that I have been working here, running into him on the floor, forced to bring bottles to his VIP room, hissing at him when he would say some non-English comment to me, I hated him. Then, only a few months ago did he show up on my doorstep with his blonde hair, blue eyes, freckled face, and forced himself deeper into my life, into my space. I still hated him. Even with the first night we experienced together, I hated that I hated him, and I hated that I wanted him. In this moment right now, I could continue to hate him for all the snarky comments he makes about me, all the side glances he throws at me, and all the problems he has caused me. Now he's snaring me with his dick into a situation that could lead to my death, but at this point, with the way he makes my body feel—as if I am being burned by a thousand matches—I would gladly walk hand in hand with him to death's doorstep.

I grab his dick, placing it on top of my panties, his pre-cum dripping onto my lace.

"Are you clean?" I moan out as he starts stroking himself against me, only a piece of fabric between us.

"Yes." His voice is so close to my ear that the tone drums against my whole body.

I tenses as I try not to orgasm. "Me too, and I'm on the—"

He rips my panties off me, throwing them over his shoulder, and slams his cock into me all the way to its hilt, not letting me get used to his size. It feels like I'm being ripped open, completely full to the breach.

"Fuck, Lily. I've wanted this for years." He slowly glides out and I can feel the ripple from all nine of his piercings. "I promise to buy you new underwear too." He leans in, kissing my cheeks. "I'll buy you everything. Anything," he says as he strokes himself back into me.

I slam my eyes shut. Feeling him inside of me is better than I could've ever imagined. He holds himself up on one arm, lying next to my head. I turn and bite his skin so I don't scream as his pace picks up speed.

"Such a good girl, taking all of me. Breathe, Lily, you can do it."

My eyes roll to the back of my head. This won't last long if he continues to talk. His accent, his voice, his lips... His hand reaches between us, circling my clit.

"Oh my god!" My toes curl and I can feel heat run throughout my body as I start convulsing. My nails dig deep into his back. I pull him closer to me, needing his body completely on top of me. I want his skin to melt into mine like

I am melting into his. His spicy scent becomes stronger, invading my nose—and that sensory overload becomes my demise. Stars burst in my vision, my mouth opening but no sound coming out.

"Let go, *álainn.* Breathe. " He continues pumping in and out of me as I try to catch my breath. His hands grab my waist, flipping me over and pointing my ass in the air. His cock enters me again and I can feel everything from his veins, to his head, to the piercings—the pain from being so sensitive to the pleasure of being so full.

"Empty your mind, *álainn*, and relax." His thrusts echo throughout the room as his skin slaps against mine. His hand wraps around my neck, squeezing and pointing my face to the ceiling. I'm bent in half and do exactly as he says—relax. His hand squeezes tightly around my neck, leaving me unable to breathe. Black spots coat my vision and I can feel drool drip from the side of my mouth, but just as I am about to pass out, his grip lessens and I suck in a breath of air.

"Can you come for me again, baby?"

"Oh god."

"He is not here right now. Just me and you, baby." He pulls out of me, flipping me around. "I want to see you."

I open my eyes to see his clear sapphire ones. He angles himself so his cock is hitting the most intense spot, pulling out almost completely before sliding back in, and repeating the process over and over again. It's torture but it's heavenly, and it doesn't take long for me to feel my orgasm burning at my skin again. I slam my eyes shut, afraid I am going to shatter and become a soulless body.

"Open your eyes, Lily. I want to see your face as you squirt all over my cock."

My eyes break open from shock and fear. He removes his body from me, standing on his knees as he presses one hand on my lower stomach and his other hand rubs my clit. My back starts to arch, and I will everything in my body to keep my eyes glued to his.

His soft eyes haven't left mine. His teeth graze against his bottom lip. "Fuck, Lily, you're so tight. *Is tú an chuisle mo chroí. Mo anama cara.*"

My body shakes, letting my orgasm take control. Jace lets go at the same time, pumping and pulsing harder until we finally become undone together,

His body partially falls on top of me, our breaths syncing with each other. I close my eyes as I try to slow my heartbeat.

Jace stands, removing his body from mine. "Stay there." He points a finger at me before walking out the door.

When he enters the room again, he has a cloth in his hand. I go to reach for it, but he pulls away. He brings the cloth to my thighs, cleaning me while leaving more kisses. He finds my shirt that was thrown across the room and helps me get situated, but I don't miss when he stuffs my ripped bra and panties in his pockets.

"I can walk," I say when he tries to pick me up off the couch.

One of his eyebrows turns upward, but he acquiesces. I swing both my feet to the ground and stand.

At least I thought I was going to stand. Both my knees buckle and Jace grabs onto me before I fully fall to the ground like a baby deer.

He sweeps me into his arms, cradling me into his chest. He walks out of the room and down the stairs out the back door, toward the underground parking.

"Wait, I have to go back to work," I say.

"Not like this you're not." Digging his keys out of his pocket, he unlocks his car door and sets me inside.

Chapter Twenty-Three

Lily

♫ "No One Knows" – Queen of the Stone Age ♫

Jace Cooks lives in a penthouse overlooking the city like the little demigod I expected him to be, but what I didn't expect was his house to be so welcoming. He has multiple plants in the corners and the cement floors are covered with plush rugs. His living room has more than one sitting area, and there's a coffee table in the middle decorated with magazines and fancy vases, as well as throw pillows and blankets. The large fireplace has candles placed along the mantel. Everything is in warm tones with different shades of green. His living room leads to the patio with floor-to-ceiling windows. The only thing missing are decorations on the walls. He needs a poster that says *I Have B.D.E. and Money.*

I stand by the window, looking at the city below. Everyone walking the streets looks so small living their own lives, dealing with their own issues. I always wonder what other people are going through. Are they about to say yes to a man they barely know and get married to him to save other women?

Probably not.

Jace comes up from behind me with two coffee mugs and he pushes his body into mine, kissing along my neck down to my shoulder. I turn around, giving him a small peck on the lips before grabbing one of the mugs.

"Are you worried?" he asks, taking a seat on one of the sofas.

I follow him, sitting on the couch, and throw one of the blankets over me. "Of course I am." The plan is insane. They want me to marry Mateo in hopes he ships me off to the mafia where I could become... I don't even know. They don't even know. They believe Mateo works for the Italian mafia, marries women, and makes them disappear. Their theory is he ships them off to Italy to become slaves or something. The only way Jace, Rowan, and Noah—who I still haven't met yet, and the person who thought of this fucking idea—will find me is with a tiny GPS that will be implanted in my toenail, secured by gel nail polish.

"I promise I will be watching you the whole time, *álainn.*"

"Like a Peregrine Falcon?" I smile into the rim of my mug.

He nods. "Like a Peregrine Falcon."

We sit in silence for a while, enjoying the coffee, until I finally have to ask. "What does, *álainn* mean?" He says it way better than I do.

He sets his coffee down on the table, walking toward me. He puts both hands on each side of my body, kissing me on the forehead. "It means beautiful." He walks away, into the open kitchen behind the living room. I follow him and watch as he takes out ingredients from his fridge.

My chest starts to ache at the fact that this whole time, I thought *álainn* was some shitty nickname, but all along—for the past three and a half years—he has been calling me beautiful.

I sit at the barstool, watching him make us sandwiches. "When did you move to New York?"

"When I was ten," he says, giving me a small smile, but it fades instantly.

"You've been in New York for forty years and you still have your accent?" I scream and duck when a slice of ham comes flying toward my face at baseball speed.

"I'm only thirty-two!" He laughs.

"A seven-year difference is pretty old." I tease.

"Well, I think my stamina is pretty good for my old age, wouldn't you agree?" He winks at me, and I can feel the heat rise to my cheeks and flow down my neck. I clench my thighs together, still feeling the soreness. He is right, his stamina is better than mine. I don't think I could go another round without having an asthma attack.

"My mother was from Dublin. My father is from New York and was visiting Dublin for work or some shit. They quickly fell in love and had me. But my father wasn't happy. He wasn't a fan of Ireland. It took him ten years to convince my mother to move to New York." He smiles, staring down at the floor. "She loved her hometown. She would tell me her childhood stories every night. I guess I kept the accent but learned the New York slang to try and fit in."

"Where is she? I would like to meet her and thank her for it."

"She died when I was twelve."

My whole body freezes. "Oh god, Jace, I'm so sorry," I reach over the counter, grabbing his arm. He shakes his head and smiles at me.

I sit back down in my seat, the air instantly shifting and becoming too quiet for me. Clearing my throat, I ask, "Did you know that Ireland has an embassy in Athens? That's where I am from, if you didn't know. My family still lives out there. And Greece has an embassy in Dublin. Coincidence for two foreigners to be put together like our hometowns. There is also some type of archaeological place in Athens about Ireland. I've never been, I've heard about it. A little. And when I was a kid, I used to see how our prime minister and president visit each other on TV. Have you ever read *The Book of Invasions*? I think I was supposed to read it in school, something about ancient Greece invading Ireland. Or was it the other way around?" I slam my mouth shut and look up to see Jace staring at me, his smile reaching his eyes. "Sorry." I shake my head, trying to clear my thoughts.

"I love it when you do that. Your little tick of your fingers and your random facts when you're nervous." He passes me a plate with a sandwich and if it wasn't for me feeling the pain of ripping my skin off from around my thumb nail, I would think I was dreaming.

The night ends after we eat our sandwiches and go over the plan multiple times. I'm not too fond of the fact that I cannot contact Jace while I wait to be kidnapped. I also am too fond on the fact that I accepted this whole idea in the first place, but I am definitely going to blame it on me being dickmatized. I thought my life was going back to normal, but obviously I spoke too soon.

It's been two weeks since I have heard from anyone. At this point, I'm nervous Mateo is going to skip the proposal part and head straight to the kidnapping. I mean, in what world would he even think I would say yes to marrying him? Especially when I practically told him to stay the fuck away from me—in a way—but these past two weeks have been an eye opener. Everything made sense—why he was constantly trying to go out with me, why he was always in my section, and why he eventually gave me a job. At any time when we were together, he could have totally offered me candy and lead me to his white stalker van. Then, boom. Lily Ballis, gone. I guess, Jace at least gave me a heads up.

Whatever Mateo plans on doing, I need him to hurry it along before I have to go back to school. What if I accidentally don't go back? What if I get shipped off to Italy and never come home? Jace never finds me, Celeste loses her best friend, I never get to own a puppy, I never get to see a gala in person, I never get to see my favorite celebrities wearing a dress I designed.

It's fine. Everything will be okay. Jace and his friends will find me.

They will find me.

I walk into the bodega, grabbing a bag of chips, and get in line. My mouth starts to water as I think about chopped turkey on a roll. I stare at the menu, trying to decide if I want a side of macaroni or cole slaw.

"I prefer the jerk chicken."

My body tenses, my mouth going from drooling like a Doberman over food to as dry as the Sonoran Desert. I slowly turn around, finding Mateo standing right behind me. He is wearing a suit that fits perfectly around his body, loafers, and glasses. I notice his dark brown hair is messy, unlike his usual pristine slicked back style. He gives me a small smile, putting his hands in his pockets and rocking back and forth on his feet. I think about what Jace told me about him, and I want to punch him in the throat. Or run away, or call the cops. Bile rises in my throat the longer I stare at him.

Remember you have to be convincing. You don't know anything, and you have to pretend to forgive and forget.

He has such a handsome face for such a fucked-up personality. I fake a smile. "Mateo, it's well to see you." I turn back around to the menu, trying not to cringe. *"Mateo, it's well to see you."* Who the fuck says that?

I can hear a chuckle behind me. "It's good to see you too, Lily. What have you been up to?"

I turn back around, looking into his eyes. I'm sure he knows what I've been up to. I have been coming to this bodega for years, and I have never seen him here and I don't think this is the side of town he likes to hang out in. "You know, just resting before school starts." I give him a small smile. This is going to be harder than it seems. How am I supposed to pretend that this man isn't making women disappear left and right? Gone without a trace, and he has no heart—no soul—to even care. I grab the hem of my shirt, twirling it in my fingers.

"I want to—" He clears his throat, looking down at his feet. "I want to apologize again. I know what I said was fucked, beyond means. I was having some business issues that night and I took it out on you. You didn't deserve it. That fucked up Mr.—" He looks back at me, smiling. "Anyway, it doesn't matter what happened that night. The only thing that matters is that I hurt your feelings, and I would really love to make it up to you."

Okay, this is it. This is my time to shine and act the part. I have seen too many TV shows, too many movies, too many celebrities interviews, to not know how to put on a show. I swallow the bile that comes up my throat, tapping my finger on my chin, and looking him up and down. I still have to pretend to be me, if this is going to work.

"And what does this 'making it up to me' insist of?"

"Well, there is a yacht part—"

"Deal. Text me the time and date." I turn around and move up in line to place my order. If I'm going to be kidnapped or fake proposed to, it might as well be on a yacht.

"Great, well, enjoy your food."

When I turn back around, he is gone. Stupid fucker was following me. He didn't come in here for food, he came in here for me. And he just proved it. How could I have been so naive about him for so long?

♫ "Bad Influence" - P!nk ♫

Murder Mateo: 6 p.m. tonight.

I stare at the text, sweat sliding down my spine. I exit the message and pull up Jace's contact.

"*Álainn*, you can't call me anymore."

"I'm going to a yacht party. What do I do? What if it happens tonight? I didn't get my toes done," I whisper into the phone, pacing around my room.

"It won't."

"How do you know?"

Jace sighs but stays silent on the other line.

"Jace?"

"I will be there," is all he says before he hangs up.

I throw my phone on the bed, looking at the outfit I picked out. I can do this.

I'm standing at the door, and just like clockwork, my doorbell rings at 6 p.m. I open it to see Mateo in a suit.

"Uh..." I look down at my tiny bikini underneath my see-through dress, leaving nothing to the imagination. "I thought you said we were going on a yacht?"

"You look perfect." He holds out his hand for me to grab. Of course I look perfect. I'm sure his nasty, murderous, kidnapping friends are going to love me. I take his hand and close my door behind me.

We drive all the way to Rhode Island in silence. For three fucking hours. With only classical music warping through the car speakers, making my ears bleed. When we reach the docks, I pull my phone out of my clutch to see a message from Jace.

Sexy Irishman: Get drunk. Have fun.

I put my phone back and step onto the large white boat. The salty breeze hits my skin as the sun sets on the horizon. The boat is full, music is already playing, and girls who are wearing less than me are dancing.

"I have some work to do at the bottom of the boat," Mateo says. "Have fun, and um... If you need me, I'll just be right down there." He points to some stairs.

I give him a smile and nod as I watch him walk down to the stairs. I turn to a waiter who has drinks on his tray and grab three glasses, downing my first one.

I hear the boat engine start and waves splash against the side of the watercraft. I take a seat on a sofa and watch as we leave the dock. If Mateo and Jace both say I should have fun, then maybe I am safe tonight. I start drinking my second glass, feeling the burn go down my throat.

Two girls start swaying toward me and plop their bodies down next to me.

"Hi," the redhead says.

"Hello."

"Why you sit by yourself?" the other girl beside me asks, stumbling over her words. She's cross-eyed as she tries to look in my direction.

"Let's take shots!" the redhead screams.

A waiter comes out of nowhere with shot glasses and tequila on a tray. The redhead grabs the whole bottle and shoos away the waiter with her hand. "I'm Mary and that's Scarlett." She points to her friend, who is now passed out next to me. Her legs are spread open, and her head hangs off the side of the couch.

"I'm Lily."

"Hi Lily, now open your mouth!" She holds up the tequila bottle, grabbing my jaw, and waterfalls it into my mouth until my cheeks fill.

I swallow all the liquor, shaking my head and slamming my eyes shut.

"Woo!" Mary screams, jumping up to stand on the couch. "I'm going to like you! Let me introduce you to everyone else."

I follow her deeper into the yacht, and she points to every girl, telling me their names. I grab the bottle from her hand and take another sip.

Hours later, we are anchored in the middle of the ocean. The sun has fully set, and the only light surrounding us is from the stars and the string lights hanging from the boat. I stand on top of a table, swaying my hips to "1 Thing" by Amerie. I haven't seen Mateo, and I don't care. Jace said he would be here, but I don't see him either. Marry and I have been taking shots back-to-back. Everyone else is surrounding us as we show off our moves.

Mary turns to me, wrapping her hands around my throat, and brings her lips to mine. I open my mouth when I taste vodka dripping from hers, and she spits it down my throat. The song ends and "Funhouse" by P!nk starts playing.

"This is my song!" I scream, jumping off the table and kicking my legs out, dancing. I can hear hoots and hollers around me as I sing along. I start strip teasing with my dress until I'm only standing in my tiny bikini. I wave my dress over my head as the beat drops and the mood changes.

Everyone joins me for the countdown in the song until the whole boat starts rocking from all of us jumping up and down.

The string lights are suddenly not the only thing illuminating us as red and blue lights begin flashing. The music stops and all the girls start screaming, running around like roaches and picking up clothes. I quickly throw my dress on and start running to where I remember Mateo was going to be. As I'm running, I see one of the girls throw white bricks off the side of the boat but is tackled to the floor by a large man.

I start trying to run faster, holding on to everything around me as the boat shakes from men boarding, tackling, and yelling at everyone to get down. Just as I am about to reach the stairs, I'm knocked to the floor on my ass.

"Hello, love."

I look up to see a large man in a uniform with a badge on his chest. He's wearing a combat helmet, a large gun wrapped around his shoulder, and a balaclava mask, only showing his eyes—his bright, piercing blue eyes.

"Jace?" I whisper.

He holds out his hand to help me off the floor. When my hand touches his, my body is jerked up into his chest. His other hand roams down my back, landing on my ass, squeezing it.

"Did you have fun?" he whispers on the side of my face.

My breathing picks up as his hand continues to roam all over my body. My knees are ready to give out when a rumble comes from his chest.

"A little too much fun, yeah?" He whips me around so that my back is pressed against his chest. He grabs both of my wrists with one hand, placing them behind me tightly, and presses something cold into my back. I look around and see men dragged from the bottom of the boat to the top, all of them with handcuffs on.

"Don't worry, Lily, I will get us out of this!" Mateo barks as he walks by me. The officer who is behind him hits him on the head with the back of his gun, telling him to keep walking.

Jace pulls me back into his chest, my body melting into his, and I can't help but let out a moan and rub my ass against him.

His face comes to the side of mine and I can feel his mask rubbing against my ear. "I think I like my little slut in handcuffs." The cold item that he was pressing into my back is removed and he brings it to my chest. I look down and my eyes widen when I see the barrel of a gun sliding between my breasts. The center between my thighs throbs for his voice. I try to lean further back on him, but my hands are keeping us apart. I wiggle my fingers to try and feel, touch, grab onto anything of his.

"Let's get you out of here." He turns us around, walking toward the end of the boat where it is dark. He unlocks my handcuffs, and I flip around to look at him. He pulls up his mask, smiling at me with those sharp teeth. I throw my hands around his neck, slamming my lips on him. I wrap my legs around his waist and throw my head back to give him access to my neck. I don't care about anything else. All I care about is having him inside me again.

I can feel us walk closer to the edge of the boat. I turn my head over my shoulder to make sure we don't fall off, and as soon as I see the dark water below us, Jace grabs my body and jumps. We land on a smaller boat—that I did not see floating in the water—with my scream echoing into the night. His lips don't leave my skin as he lays me down and hovers over me.

He starts to unbuckle his combat cargo pants and pulls his balaclava mask back down. He grabs my dress, pulling it up to my neck and pulls my bikini bottoms to the side. He slowly slides into me, letting every inch build pressure into my core. A gasp leaves my mouth when he grabs me by the shoulders, pressing me down into him, completely filling me.

With every thrust, the small boat rocks back and forth, ocean water spilling all around us. He picks up his pace and I can't help but moan into the dead of night.

My cries are quickly silenced when Jace grabs his handgun and shoves it into my mouth. My heart crashes against my chest as I go cross-eyed looking at my lips wrapped around the cold metal barrel. He grabs the nape of my neck, pulling me closer to his face. "Quiet, my little slut. You don't want your boyfriend to know his girlfriend is getting fucked on a boat right next to him."

His thrusts become harder as he lets out a growl. My mouth spreads wide from the gun being shoved further down my throat. Tears prickle at my eyes and drool slips down my cheeks.

I'm insane. This is insane. Yet my body can't help but want more. The pain from the gun being down my throat, his mask only showing his eyes, his piercings rippling in my center... All of it is creating a fucking catastrophe of emotions within me.

He lifts me up, letting me straddle him as I bounce up and down on his cock. It's like I can't stop, my nerve endings inflaming against my skin.

He removes the gun from my mouth and points it under my chin. "Look at the stars, Lily. Not even the stars compare to you." One of his hands grabs ahold of my hips as he continues to keep the barrel pressed against my chin, forcing me to stare up into the sky. Our skin slaps against each other like waves crashing onto shore.

I can't take it anymore, feeling the shivers run up my legs into the pit of my stomach. I open my mouth, crying when my orgasm takes over. Jace lays me back down on my back, shoves his gun down my throat, and slams himself into me repeatedly. My wails are muted against the gun as he keeps my orgasm continuing with every thrust. I watch as his finger roams toward the trigger, sweat dripping down my forehead and my blood running cold. I grab at his hand to try to remove the gun from my mouth, but he only presses deeper into my throat.

My vision goes black as I feel Jace release inside me with a grunt as he simultaneously pulls the trigger. My eyes shut, and for a second, I believe I am dead. Until I feel the gun being removed from my mouth and his breath blowing against my cheek.

"Asshole!" I scream, pushing his body off me.

He laughs, pulling up his mask and kissing me on the cheek. "Never played Russian roulette, baby?"

"You're insane," I snap, but in reality, I have never felt more alive.

Chapter Twenty-Four

Lily

One Month Later...

♫ "Touchin' Me" - Chandler Leighton ♫

I sit in Celeste's room, staring at all her boxes. "Girl, you sure about this?" I ask. She turns to me, putting her hands on her hips, and tips her head to the side. This is my third time asking her today, but I can't help but worry.

"Lily, I am only moving in." She laughs and shakes her head, continuing to put her art supplies into boxes.

"Yeah, but you do know, once you move in, then comes a baby and then comes a wedding," I say. I know it's usually the other way around, but we live in the twenty-first century. We all know pregnancy ends up coming first.

"I don't think that's how the saying goes."

I can feel the pressure behind my eyes, my ears becoming muffled as I watch her continue to pack. My best friend is moving in with her psycho boyfriend and I will be left here alone. I haven't told her about the plan with Mateo, scared that she will make me back out of it, or worse, that she won't leave my side. This could be the last time I ever see her, and she doesn't even know it.

"Lil, I swear. Don't you cry."

She holds her arms out, enticing me to give her a hug, which makes me burst into tears. My best friend, Celeste Jones, is giving me a free hug. The woman who hates physical touch and always pats my head when I engage her in any type of intimacy, is offering *me* a hug. I run to her, wrapping my arms around her tiny body, and cry into her shoulder.

"You know Lily, we have an extra room. You can come stay with us and drop this nasty house."

I turn to see Rowan standing at the door. Fucker. He knows what's going on and knows I can't leave since I probably only have one more month of freedom before I become Mrs. Davenport.

Celeste releases me from a hug, letting me wipe the tears from my face. "Ew, gross. I do not want to hear you guys have sex every night." I put my hands on my hips, pointing to Rowan. "I swear, if you do not take care of her, I am going to break into your house and strangle you in your sleep with a shoelace."

Rowan doesn't respond to my threat. He walks away from the door and kisses Celeste on her forehead before picking up another box.

"I can continue paying my half of the rent so you don't have to find a new roommate."

"Oh god no. You're a grown-up now. Go live your life." I give her a smile, leaning down to tape up another box. I won't be living here much longer anyway. Or living at all, for that matter. I wish I could tell her. "I have to grow up at some point. Or I'll just find someone else to tell me when to eat and sleep. Oh!" I pause, taping the box. "Maybe I will find me a professional chef to be a roommate."

She holds her hands in the air again. Two hugs in one day? Someone please call an ambulance, I might have a heart attack. I jump off the floor and embrace my best friend.

"These are all of them, yeah?"

My body tenses at the sexy, sultry voice that's just entered the room. Celeste pulls back from the hug and I put my hands in my short pockets, looking down at my feet to make sure I don't melt into the ground.

"Yes, those are it. Thank you," Celeste says.

I hear footsteps leave the room and when I look up, I see the back of Jace. His hair is wildly blonde, like the sun leaned down to kiss him on top of his head as a baby, gifting him with the color. The last time I saw him, he was decked out in a county sheriff's uniform while he fucked my brains out and almost *blew my brains out,* in the middle of the ocean. When he finished, he told me I couldn't call him or see him but that he would contact me when he has more information. All I want to do is rush to him and wrap my body around him, never letting go. Again, blaming all this on being dick-matized.

I grab my arm when Celeste pinches me. "Ouch!"

"Did you guys fuck when I was in Italy?"

"What?! No!"

She shakes her head, grabbing her purse, and walks out her bedroom door. I follow her out, standing on our stairs, and watch as she gets into the moving truck with Rowan. I see Jace's car parked right behind the truck. I wave to Celeste, watching the truck pull into the street. My head snaps when I see Jace hasn't left. I pull out my phone from my back pocket when I feel it vibrate.

Unknown: Open bedroom window.

My bedroom window is nailed shut, how am I supposed to do that? I shut the front door behind me, walking to my room to see a new window installed with double locks.

What the hell? When does he do these things?

I open the window to see Jace come around the corner, walking up with my neighbor's garbage bin. He jumps on top of it and through my window like a cat.

"I have missed you so much." He grabs my face with both of his hands, kissing me like he has been deprived for years.

I follow his lead, rubbing my fingers through his locks and wrapping my legs around his body. He backs us into my bed and climbs on top of me.

"I thought you said I had to be a good little girl for Mateo," I squeal while rashly grabbing his shirt to pull it over his head so I can feel his cold skin on my fingertips.

"You can be a good little girl for him. But I need you to be a bad girl for me." He pulls my shirt up, biting my nipple and pulling it through his teeth. He reaches with one hand, unzipping my shorts, and shoves his fingers to my clit. "Fuck, look at you." He brings his fingers between us before sucking the juices off and rubs the remaining across my lips. His open smile shows off his sharp teeth and his pink swollen lips.

He moves his body to the end of me, taking my shorts with him and rips my panties in half *again.* "I promise I'm keeping count. I'll buy you new ones." His warm breath reaches my slit and licks every inch of me.

My back arches to the sky as his tongue darts out, flicking my clit. I grab at his hair, pulling to try and keep my body from releasing.

"I can't go that long again," he says as he bites at the sensitive spot inside my thigh. "I'm addicted, *álainn*." He returns to fucking me with his tongue, and every time I feel like I am about to come, he stops. "I might fuck up the whole plan just because I can't stay away."

My lower stomach tightens at the sound of him, the smell of him. Everything about him. My toes curl when I hear his belt and zipper coming undone. I watch as he wraps his belt together into two loops, grabs my hands, and shoves them through, tightening it. The leather cuts at my skin as he moves my arms above my head and secures me to my bedframe.

"I'm losing my fucking mind. I need to see you night and day. From when I wake up in the morning to when I kiss you before bed. I want to see you walk around naked after I fuck you in every position possible." His mouth kisses every spot of my body that has never been kissed. "I want to taste you every hour." Kiss. "Every minute." Kiss. "Every goddamn second." Kiss.

He says he is losing his mind, but my mind is being sent to another universe. Never has any man confessed the words Jace is producing right now. My body melts under his skin. It responds to his touch, it craves him.

"I want you all to myself," are the last words he says before both my moans and his grunts fill the air as he shoves his cock into me. His hand cups the top of my head to stop me from banging against my headboard as he drives into me. There is no oxygen left in my lungs as every last one of my breaths is taken away.

We lie in my bed, breathing hard, dazed, sweaty, and worn out. All my pillows and blankets are scattered on the floor. Jace's body takes up more than half my bed, spreading out his limbs as I lie on top of him. I can feel his dick still hard against my stomach while I wrap myself around him like a pretzel.

"If you had a redo button on your life, would you press it?" I say, breaking the silence.

"No." His fingers run through my tangled hair, softly brushing them out.

"Why not?"

"I would have never met you."

"You barely know me, Jace," I laugh, outlining his tattoos with my fingers. "What if I was some type of psycho killer?"

"I would happily die by your hand if that meant I didn't have to live without you."

I lift my body from his, placing my hand on my heart. "Jace Cook, are you professing your love to me?"

"Did me fucking you to oblivion not say enough?" He rolls over me, trapping me underneath him as his cock finds my entrance as if they were two magnets. "You're the only person I want to fuck in this lifetime and the next."

"So poetic," I moan, while he grabs my ass, squeezing as he pushes into me for the second time today. How this man has this much stamina truly inspires me. Every part of my body is so sensitive it's painful, yet my mind welcomes it like no other.

It doesn't take long for my eyes to blur as a rainbow light show fills my vision. My body rocks to connect with his speed, feeling him pulse inside me. He holds his weight on his elbows while he catches his breath before kissing me on the forehead and jumping off the bed. My eyes follow his cute plump butt as he walks toward my bathroom.

He comes back a second later, standing at the edge of my bed with a washcloth in hand. "I think your new name is apple strudel."

"What, why?" I ask, my eyes following his finger as it points straight at my center. "Gross, no!"

He breaks out into a laugh, climbing back on the bed. "You don't like that one, yeah? How 'bout Twinkie? Jelly donut?"

"Stop!" I push his body off me as he continues laughing. "You're ruining so many desserts, and that washcloth is not going to cut it." I swing my legs over my bed, heading toward my bathroom to turn the shower on. I can feel cum dripping down my thighs and some of it is already drying against my skin. I step into the shower, the hot water burning against my skin and around my wrist where I was tied to the bed.

"I got you another phone."

I almost slip in the shower from turning around too fast. Jace catches me by my waist to keep me still. I don't know how he moves so swiftly and quietly. He grabs my body soap from my hands, squirting it into the washcloth and rubbing it against my body. I close my eyes, enjoying the feeling of his hands as they explore.

"What for?" I ask.

"The phone will be for me and you to communicate only. No one else." He places the washcloth outside my shower, grabs my shampoo bottle, and threads his fingers through my hair. "I already could have fucked up by texting you, also with me being here. But I just couldn't—"

"Live without me. I know." I place my hand on his cheek, feeling his stubble against my palm. A part of me is being sarcastic, but it almost feels like I'm not lying. Jace is truly obsessed with me and has been for years, and maybe… just maybe, I have been growing feelings for him too.

He slaps my ass and pushes me further back under the water. "I also shouldn't be telling you this because Rowan thinks you're going to fuck it up... but we think the proposal is coming sooner than later. We found shit on the boat the other night. Plane tickets, money..."

My breath hitches, the warm water turning cold against my skin. Jace told me that night that all those girls I met were being targeted as well. He told me they were all safe now, but most of the men were booked and released. The raid was just a ploy for information. Jace and Rowan jumped on a Coast Guard boat to come find me. Jace was there to rescue me while Rowan went snooping around.

"I promise. I will find you," he says, grabbing my body and pressing it against his.

Chapter Twenty-Five

Jace

♫ "Cherry Waves" - Deftones ♫

I place a kiss on her forehead and pull the blanket over her shoulders. I walk to her desk, pulling my chip out of her computer, and place it in my jeans pocket. I made a coding program specifically designed for her so that I can constantly see what she searches on the web. With it, I'm able to see everything she does on the computer. I like to make sure everything I buy her is exactly what she wants. It was also how I was able to log into her school account and pay off her tuition. Yeah, the coding program is too high tech for her computer, makes it run a little slow, and at times my program will pop up and show my codes to her. But she doesn't know what it is, and I doubt she is curious enough to research. She just blames it on her computer being old.

I make sure to lock the window on my phone app after I climb out of it. This is my third night in a row that I have been in her room, watching her sleep. She has been doing well at pretending with Mateo. He has been taking her out more often, but everywhere they go, I am there in the shadows, watching. The sun will soon rise, and she will have a random lady at her door ready to attach a GPS chip in her pedicure.

I pull my hood above my head, walking to my car. When I get in, all I can do is sit there. Lily is about to marry someone who is not me, and I don't like it one feckin' bit.

Noah stands on Rowan's patio smoking a cigarette. "Back so soon? Couldn't get enough of me, huh?"

"Careful, your ego is almost as big as mine," I say, walking to the front door. When I turn the knob, Noah jumps in front of me, blocking the door.

"I wouldn't go in there if I were you."

"Why?" I'm really not in the mood for games.

His points a thumb over his shoulder at the door. "They've been going at it for hours."

I run my hands along my face, turning around and going to sit on the steps. I can hear Noah's boots against the wood panels before he plops himself next to me.

"You look like shit." He takes a drag of his cigarette, blowing it into the wind.

"Gee, yeah, thanks man."

"You worried?"

I turn my head toward him. I swear this kid is getting bigger by the day. I don't blame him. All he can do is watch the property and indulge in the private gym that used to be Rowan's basement—where we did most of our work. Now I have to drag bodies across town to the abandoned warehouse. We've been so focused on Mateo's case we haven't taken anyone else. But this is big, bigger than what we are used to, and we have to focus. This isn't our typical PI case. This is something the FBI should be working on, but that could take years, and we don't have years. Women are going missing and the only ones who are ready for the action—is us.

I refuse to let this be another Joan case. But the dread that ate us alive for years on end, not knowing what happened, could have been solved if we just opened our feckin' eyes. Opened our eyes to see who was standing right in front of us, who knew more than we did.

I need another plan just in case the current one goes to shit. I can't have Lily legally bonded to Mateo. I don't *want* Lily bonded to Mateo.

"What do you know about marriages?" I ask.

"What kind of question is that?" He pulls out a joint from behind his ear, sticking it in his mouth and lighting it.

"Fuck, I don't know. Does there need to be witnesses and that man who speaks from the Bible and shit?"

Noah starts coughing, his bushy eyebrows scrunching together when he turns to look at me. "What the fuck are you asking me right now?"

I jump off the stairs and walk into Rowan's house. Noah following right behind me. I catch a glimpse of Celeste wrapped in bedsheets walking down the foyer into another room. Rowan cuts the corner, skipping down the stairs with his shorts hanging low on his hips.

"Jesus, ever heard of boxers?" Noah turns away, heading into the kitchen.

"Nobody asked you to be here." Rowan flips a finger at Noah.

I know Rowan hates Noah here, but they are turning more into siblings, creating this fucked up *Three Brothers* situation we have going on. I grab onto Rowan's shoulders from the back. "I've got an idea, and you might feckin' hate it."

"Is this going to require me to have a fucking cigarette?" he asks, turning around and scowling at me already.

My hands drop from his shoulders. "Oh, feckin' hell." I pinch the bridge of my nose, taking a deep breath. "Probably."

"Noah!" Rowan screams, holding out his hand toward Noah, who is only two feet away.

After I told Rowan and Noah about my second plan, Celeste begged me to stay for dinner. I knew I was going to like this girl the day she came and dropped off a feast for Rowan as a thank-you for saving her in Athens. That night, she stared at all of us, scared shitless. Her face was pale, and her brown eyes lost its color when she saw Rowan, John, and I covered in blood from head to toe. She lost her appetite, and I gained mine for her delicious cooking.

We all sit gathered around the dining table, no one saying a word as we shove Celeste's home-cooked meal down our throats. Celeste slowly eats with a smile on her face as she watches all of us eat like men on their first day out of prison.

"I'm assuming you guys like it? It was a new recipe, so I was a little nervous."

Rowan stands from his seat, kissing the top of her head and heading to the kitchen for seconds.

"If I keep eating your meals, I am going to need more equipment for the downstairs gym," Noah says with his mouth full.

"Good—" Celeste's eyes go wide, her hand slamming against her mouth. Her chair scrapes on the marble floor when she jumps out of her seat and runs to the stairs. I turn around in my seat to see Rowan's face stripped of color as his eyes follow Celeste's movements. His body finally unfreezes, and he runs upstairs to follow her. I turn toward Noah and he shrugs his shoulders as he continues to eat.

Minutes later, footsteps echo on the stairs. I turn around to see Celeste peeking her head around the corner. "Sorry. I think I caught a bug. You guys finish dinner and have a good night."

"Feel better," Noah says as he pushes his plate away, rubbing at his stomach.

Rowan rubs Celeste's back from behind and kisses the top of her head before she dashes away.

"Caught a bug, yeah?" I say to Rowan as he grabs our plates off the table and walks to the kitchen.

"Yeah, seems so."

I stand from my seat, walking to the other end of the kitchen island. "You think this bug happens to come with two legs, two arms, ten toes, and ten fingers?" A big smile spreads across my face when Rowan drops a plate, sending glass shards across the floor. Behind me, Noah breaks into a laugh while coughing up a storm. "Says things like 'Mama' and 'Papa'?" I pinch my lips together, holding in my laugh as Rowan's eyes turn molten.

He bends down to pick up pieces of the broken plate. "No. I'm sure she is just not feeling well."

"You sure 'bout that? Y'all continue to fuck like rabbits every day, sooner or later, consequences are bound to happen," Noah comments when he finally catches his breath.

Rowan stands up, putting his hands on the kitchen island with his head between his shoulders. "I'm not ready," he whispers.

I wipe the smile from my face, walking to stand by him and placing my hand on his shoulder. "Nobody ever is. But you guys will be great parents."

"Actually..." Noah starts walking toward us, shaking his head. "Let's not jump to conclusions. I'd rather not have to watch over Rowan, Celeste, and a mini-Celeste. I didn't sign up for daycare."

"Who says it won't be a mini-Rowan?" I smirk at Noah, my mood changing again at the thought of our family growing. Rowan and I may not be blood related, but he is the only one I consider family. Now we have Celeste, Lily, and fuck, I have to include Noah too. Our family just continues to grow.

"Shut the fuck up, both of you." Rowan storms out of the kitchen, the balls of his feet slamming against the stairs. Noah and I turn toward each other, shaking our heads.

Chapter Twenty-Six

Lily

♫ "Underneath It All (ft. Lady Shaw)" - No Doubt ♫

Have you ever had a woman come to your house, set up a station, and give you a pedicure in your living room? I bet not. This is the type of thing you get done when you're wealthy and entitled. I watch as the lady paints my toes black. "Do you do this a lot?"

"Put GPS chips in women's pedicures? No."

Her attitude reminds me of Roxxie, always responding with a short, angry tone, which makes things so incredibly awkward. The nail tech has bleach blonde hair cut into a bob, and light hazel eyes. She's gorgeous but her attitude stinks.

I grab the phone that Jace gave me. I never don't have it on me, checking it every ten minutes to see if he's texted me. Especially after his insane confession of wanting to be with me every day. It sent an unknown emotion swirling through my body. I don't know if it's fight or flight. I shake my head and give in to text him.

Me:

Who hired her? She is kinda mean?

Not a Sexy Irishman:
Rowan.

I laugh when his name pops up. Jace's contact in my personal phone is "Sexy Irishman," so I figured putting "Not a Sexy Irishman" in this phone was fitting.

Me:

Well, that makes sense. Rowan has the personality of a warthog. She is definitely the type of woman he would hire.

Not a Sexy Irishman:
And how do you know what a warthog's is?   personality is?

Me:

All warthogs do is huff and run. The same thing Rowan did to Celeste when he dropped her back off at our doorstep after Italy.

Not a Sexy Irishman:

Got jokes, *álainn*?

If there was a camera in the house right now, I'm sure I look so stupid staring and smiling at my phone like a little teenage girl.

Not a Sexy Irishman:

It's on. I can see your location.

The more days that have passed, the more nervous I get. This sick feeling in the pit of my stomach... The "what ifs" lingering in my brain like sticky little worms...

"You're all done."

I look down at my pedicure. It looks completely normal, and not like I have a tiny GPS tracker in my left big toe. "Thank you, I—" When I look up, she is already heading toward the front door.

Okay then.

I lie back down on the couch, staring at Jace's last message.

Me:

How do you think he is going to do it?

"Kidnap you? Or propose to you?"

I jump up to see Jace standing in my bedroom door frame. "Jesus Christ, how did you get in?"

He shrugs his shoulders, walking toward me. He picks up my legs and throws them over his thighs as he sits down. "How do I think he is going to do what?" he asks again.

"Propose. I don't think I want to know the kidnapping part." I wince.

His hands roam over my feet, slightly threading my arches. "I'm sure it will be public. He wants the attention."

I grab one of my throw pillows, covering my face with it. I would rather die gagging on my own throw-up than have a public proposal. Everyone clapping for you, congratulating you... It's a form of attention I'd rather not have.

I throw the pillow off me. "What if Celeste finds out?" She will murder me for not telling her.

"She won't. Rowan is keeping her busy." Jace winks at me, showing his bright, cutting smile. I grab the pillow off the floor and throw it at his head. We break out into a wrestling match when he jumps on top of me, pinning down my arms. I'm laughing and screaming as his cold hands run against my skin, trying to find all my ticklish spots.

Someone please hide the cameras. I'm acting like a teenager in her first relationship.

Our bodies freeze when my doorbell rings, and the house becomes eerily silent as Jace and I stare at each other. I kick Jace off me, running to the door, and look out the peephole to see Mateo standing outside. I run back down the hallway, mouthing to Jace, "It's Mateo."

Jace calmly gets off the couch and walks into my bedroom, as if this could not affect everything. I walk back to the door, straighten my shirt, pat down my hair, and wipe my clammy hands along my shorts.

"Hey, Mateo."

He leans in, giving me a kiss on both of my cheeks. I try not to gag at the action and put a smile on my face as he leans back.

"What was all that noise?" His eyebrows pinch together as he looks beyond his glasses. Glasses that I once thought cute, but now all I see is a fucking devil in disguise.

"Sorry, I must have had the TV volume too high if you could hear it from out there." I laugh to hide behind my lie.

"You going to invite me in?"

No. No. No. God, no. I don't want you in my fucking house, or my fucking life. And I hope you die a terrible, painful death with Icy Hot shoved up your asshole.

I move my body to the side, letting him in.

"Babe. How long have you been living here? You should have told me this is what you go through." His eyes wander throughout my living room. My gaze mimics his, looking at the leather sofa that, yeah, may have gone through some rough patches, and the coffee table that me and Celeste bought from a thrift store and broke on the subway back home. Our TV stand is a cubicle I'm sure is meant for shoes. But it's home. My home. Mine and Celeste's home. I have memories here and I'm proud of it. So how dare he judge?

"It's not all bad." I jump onto the couch, tucking my legs under me. I wish I could shove his balls back up his stomach. If I meet his mother and father at the wedding, I want to tell them what a horrible child they have raised, and they should be embarrassed.

Who am I kidding? He obviously got his personality from someone. I watch as he carefully sits down at the edge of my couch like he might catch a disease if he gets too comfortable.

"Right... So, I was wondering if you would like to go out to dinner tonight?"

Like a dog, my ears perk up at the sound of two taps from my bedroom wall. Oh god, is Jace still here? If Mateo decides to be noisy, we will be so fucked. Plan over. But Mateo obviously didn't hear since he is still staring at me with the fakest smile I have ever seen. His upper lip twitches when we don't break eye contact. I really thought I knew how to read people but boy, was I wrong. And my theory about psychopaths was right—the true psychopaths pretend to be nice to you before they murder you. The crazy people who just show you they are psycho from the beginning are just "normal" people. Humans. With human emotions. Ever since Jace told me the truth about Mateo, I see right through him. Memories of us in the subway resurface like pictures floating through my head. The nights at the club where I would sit and talk to him... All of it was a front.

"Actually, I'm sorry. I have to get a head start on the school syllabus."

He nods as he stands from the couch, his hand rubbing my arm and creating goosebumps along my skin. And not the good kind of goosebumps. It's the kind you get when you want to shake off the invisible bug you have crawling on you. The goosebumps you get when you see something so sickening you want to rip your skin off your bones.

"No worries. I am so proud of you, babe. You work so hard."

I might need muscle relaxers after holding this smile for so long. His face leans closer to mine. His eyes roam to my lips before coming back to my eyes. My heart rate picks up and my fingers start to twitch. Fuck, he is about to kiss me. If I twitch or lean back, it will destroy everything. My heart is pounding against my chest, begging my sternum to open so it can hop away.

Mateo stops when we hear a car alarm going off. He turns his head, and I let out the breath I was holding deep in my chest.

"That sounds like mine." He takes off toward my front door and I follow right behind him.

Jace, please don't be out here.

Parked in front of my house is Mateo's BMW with a brick in the rear window. Mateo pulls his keys out of his pocket and turns off the alarm. "Son of a bitch!" he yells, picking up the brick and throwing it into the distance. "I'm getting you out of this neighborhood. It's not safe." He points at me before getting into his car and driving away.

I run inside, closing the door behind me, and let my head fall back against it. My hand is plastered to my chest, feeling my heart beating a mile a minute.

"Sorry. I couldn't let it happen tonight."

I look down my hallway to see Jace standing there. The light from my living room shining behind him, highlighting every portion of his body. A demigod. A fucking demigod.

My demigod.

"A brick?" I chuckle.

He walks toward me, his eyes never leaving mine. "He's lucky I didn't throw one at his face." He grabs the nape of my neck, pressing his lips against mine, and picks me up to walk us back toward the couch.

Chapter Twenty-Seven

Lily

♫ "Bring Me to Life" - Evanescence ♫

I finally agreed to meet with Mateo for dinner. I couldn't hide out any longer and needed to get this over with. My palms are clammy as I hold the expensive leather menu in my hands, pretending to understand any of these words on the paper. I mean, seriously? Do they add gold flakes to the food? Why is everything so expensive?

The waiter comes over to drop off a bottle of wine and explains something about how long it has aged and the taste of it. I couldn't care less. Hand me the dyed Red 40 grape juice from a box and I will slurp it down if it will make me intoxicated right now.

The waiter asks if we are ready to order—which I am not—but Mateo decides to take it into his own hands and order for both of us. If he was going to do that, he could have warned me, so I didn't spend twenty minutes trying to figure out how to pronounce *bouillabaisse*.

I grab the wine glass, holding it to my lips before taking one large gulp. I sit through our appetizer, which consists of three cherry tomatoes cut in half with mozzarella and a leaf in the middle. Then for our entrees, Mateo gets some type of protein while I sit here and stare at my rabbit food—a piece of lettuce with a stick and a side of lemon wedge.

I can't wait to go home and order take-out.

Then comes dessert. I stare at my chocolate fondue cake that holds a ring right in the middle. I stare at it, unable to process. I knew this was coming, yet I'm still in shock. I turn to my left to see him on one knee, and look around the dimly lit restaurant to see people staring and holding out their phones.

"Lily, I know this is fast, but I have loved you—"

I pinch the skin on the back of my thighs. This is the only thing I can think of to make this seem real. Tears start to prick at the corners of my eyes.

Jace and Rowan owe me big fucking time. This is so embarrassing.

"—since the day I first saw you at the club. Will you marry me?"

Not only is this embarrassing, but it is also the lamest proposal I have ever heard. But me, being the good actress I am, nod animatedly, letting the tears roll down my face. People start clapping around us and Mateo stands off the floor, hugging me, and somehow, I slip up and miss that his face has moved, and he kisses me on the lips.

Note to self: bleach my mouth when I get home.

He finally sits down, taking a big inhale like it was the hardest thing he has ever had to do in his life. His smile reaches for the stars, and it's just as terrifying as Art the Clown.

He pulls the slice of cake toward him, pulling out the ring and wiping the chocolate off before he puts the big rock on my finger. It barely fits, leaning to the side. It's truly sad to think how other woman have fallen for this. But that is the goal here. To find out where these women are going and how we can stop it. I have to keep that in mind when I am being thrown in a rapist's van at some point in the next couple of weeks.

Take me to the Bat Cave, I am now a vigilante.

Thankfully, after dinner, Mateo drops me off at my house without protesting to take me to his place, or him inviting himself into mine to celebrate. His excuse is he has to go into the office to get some work done. When I get in, I see Jace sitting on my couch, watching *True Blood* from the first season while eating popcorn. His dark blue jeans and tight white T-shirt fit his skin like everything was made specifically for him.

His head turns when he hears the clack of my heels against the hardwood floor. "You did so good." He leaves the couch, walking to me.

"You saw?" I reach down, taking off my kitten heels.

"Of course I did. The tears really sold it. I didn't know you knew how to cry on command."

I turn my body away from him, looking over my shoulder and pointing to the back of my thigh just beneath the hem of my dress to where a big red mark stains my skin. "I was pinching myself the whole time."

Jace gets on his knees, kissing the welts. His hands grab both of my thighs to force my whole body closer to him. "Maybe you should be an actress instead of a lawyer." His kisses roam higher up my thigh, and he pulls my dress up, leaving more kisses on my ass.

"I would choose to be anything besides a lawyer."

He turns me around and stands up to his full height. I lean up to look at his scrunched, confused face.

"You don't want to be a lawyer?"

I walk away to set my purse down on the coffee table before swinging my body onto the couch. "Nope," I say, extenuating the P with a popping sound.

Jace kneels besides me, his hand finding all my nerve endings again. "Then why are you going to school for it?"

My hands slap against my face before I run them down over my eyes, probably smearing my makeup. "Fuck. Jace. I am so sorry. I forgot you paid for my semester. I still promise to pay you back, it's just that—" I stop and sit up from the couch. My knees hit his chest since he's still on the floor. "Actually, no. Me marrying Mateo *is* the payback. I no longer owe you."

Jace stands from the floor, pushing my body back into the couch and bending closer to me. "I never expected nor want you to pay me back for anything. In fact, I owe you for doing this for us. Which I plan to make up to you for the rest of your life." His lips find the center of my neck, leaving kisses along the sensitive area. "But first." His hands wrap underneath me, pulling me up and flipping me around so I sit on top of him. "Why don't you want to be a lawyer?"

I lay my head on his shoulder. He smells like fresh wood, mixed with an amber or dark cherry. I close my eyes inhaling it. "I couldn't disappoint my parents."

He is quiet for a moment before he asks, "So, what would Miss Ballis like to do with her life instead?" His fingers roam along my back, soothing me. My eyes close, savoring the feeling. "I want to design fashion. Be a fashion designer."

"My wife is a fashion designer. I like the sound of that."

I lift my head off his shoulder. "Excuse me, sir. Wife? I am currently engaged, if you have forgotten. Who said there was going to be an *us*?" I tease about being engaged, but I can feel my heart pounding at the fact that he called me his wife.

"You're mine, Lily Ballis. From the very beginning you have been mine. Always will be mine. I don't care if you hate me, I don't care if you're engaged or married. If we were not in the situation we are in right now, and you got married to someone else, some low-life cunt, I would make you a widow. From the first time you bumped into me at the club and stared at me with your beautiful, big green eyes, you have been mine."

Tears bundle in my eyes, and this time they are real. I don't know how we ended up here. I don't know how or when Jace cracked open my heart and stole it for himself. I can't keep pretending that this man hasn't been in the back of my mind for months. He can still be annoying, he can still infuriate me, but he truly is the kindest man I have ever encountered. I think about all the times I have been mean to him, yet all he has ever done is stare at me with hope and fondness in his clear blue eyes. All he has ever done is show me my worth. And now, I never want to let him go.

Chapter Twenty-Eight

Lily

♫ "Nothing Else Matters" - Metallica ♫

I stand in the mirror looking at the white wedding dress hanging off my body. Nobody is in the building besides my bridal stylist and me. Celeste still has no idea what is going on, and I refuse to invite anyone I know to this wedding. I made an excuse to Mateo that my parents can't fly into the States, and he didn't ask any questions. Obviously, because he doesn't care. I am just a paycheck to his sick fucking mind.

This is the third dress I have tried on. I don't care for any of them. I don't care which one I pick since none of it matters. But something in my head wants to try on every single dress in the building, praying that one day, I can enjoy this. In another lifetime, I can put a dress on and walk down the aisle with my father at my side, tears streaming down my face and my smile brighter than the sun.

In another lifetime.

"Oh no, no. Let me go get the tissues." My bridal stylist runs to a table, handing me the box. "I would cry too if I was wearing that dress. You look beautiful," she says.

I give her a smile, dotting the tissues underneath my eyes. The dress is cut in a low V with sheer sleeves and a drop down in the back. The train is short, and the fabric tightens all the way to my hips before flaring out.

"I will take it. Help me out of it, please." I can feel my skin melting off my bones the more I stare at the dress.

"We will do the touch-up and call you when it's ready." She stands behind me on the podium, unzipping the back awkwardly.

I would get awkward too if I heard my monotone voice. This is supposed to be a time of joy, friends, laughter, and champagne. But instead, I am here alone at 8 p.m. on a Tuesday, crying by myself. I get out of the dress quicker than I put it on. Thanking the stylist for her time, I hand her Mateo's credit card he gave me for the wedding and walk out the shop. I head into New York's crowd, toward the subway station. My phone vibrates in my hand and when I look at it, I quickly wipe away the tears that have fallen down my cheeks.

Not a Sexy Irishman:
Go to Woodster St.

I pull up my phone's map to see it's only across the street. I walk down an alley to a cul-de-sac and see Jace's car parked in the dark corner. I quickly jump in, and he takes off before I even have my seatbelt buckled.

"Where are we going?" I hold onto the door handle, watching as he serves through traffic heading to Holland Tunnel, which is the complete opposite way to Brooklyn.

"Anywhere but here."

His hands grip the steering wheel, turning white. I softly lay my hand on top of his thigh, which causes his head to snap my direction. His eyes glow almost white from the streetlights, his Adam's apple bobbing up and down. Once. Twice.

"Jace, we can't keep doing this. I don't want to do this as much as you don't want me to." I shake my head. "But at night, I can't stop imagining all the other women. All the women we could be helping now and in the future." At first, I was hesitant about this whole situation—their accusations about what is happening, what is going on, and who is involved. Then I came to my senses and realized this shit *does* happen. People get kidnapped every day and disappear without a trace. It doesn't just happen in movies, or on TV. Life is not all butterflies and rainbows, unicorns jumping out of clouds. Life is a fucked-up journey we all have to endure and sometimes people get the shitty end of the stick. Their lives are turned upside down in the blink of an eye just because some people are sick and fucking twisted. If I can somehow try to make a difference—especially when I know who is doing it, especially when I am in the middle of the damn circle—I will. Without a doubt.

Jace face finally turns back to the road, thankfully so we don't crash.

"I found your drawings. You're good. I think you should go to Fashion school."

I huff out a laugh. "Yeah, tell that to my parents."

"I will when you invite me to Athens."

I catch on to him changing the subject. Every time we are near each other, he talks about the future, and I know it's just him adding light to the situation. Avoiding the "what ifs." "I hope you like kids, because my brothers and sisters are handfuls." I shake my head, remembering that the last time I spoke to my mother, she was still yelling at them to share their toys.

"Do you want kids?" He quickly turns to me before looking back at the road, then he makes a U-turn, heading back in the direction of my house.

"Yeah, I want twelve." I shrug my shoulders and turn to look at all the cars through the window, hiding my smile.

"Then it looks like I need a bigger house."

I turn back to him. "And horses, and cows, and chickens, and donkeys."

"Then I guess I need a farm." He covers my hand and squeezes. His thumb finds my cheek, wiping away another tear I didn't know had fallen. "Lily, I promise—"

"I know. You will find me."

Chapter Twenty-Nine

Lily

One Month Later...

♫ "Lonely Day" - System of A Down ♫

I can hear people walking down the hall, laughing and talking. I sit in the chair while some lady does my makeup, and another woman does my hair. My eye shadow has hints of purple, making my green eyes pop. My hair is being curled before it gets wrapped half up, half down. The room is silent as I watch them get me dressed for this fake wedding. Even after my stylists leave, I continue to sit at the vanity, staring at myself in the mirror.

I turn my head when I hear two knocks at the door. "Come in." My eyes bulge when I see Jace squeeze his body through the door, quickly locking it behind him. "What are you doing here?!"

He walks up to me, grabbing my face, and plants a deep kiss on my lips, his tongue swirling with mine. My hand reaches out, grabbing onto his suit jacket to pull him in deeper.

"I was invited," he says when he pulls away.

"Who else is here?" I look around as if someone is going to jump out of the corner. Oh god, if Celeste is here, she is going to burn this church down.

"Just me, Noah, and Axel. Rowan is at home with Celeste." His mouth crashes to my exposed neck, finishing his sentence by sucking on my skin.

I try to push him off, but my arms have been replaced with noodles. The sensation of his soft lips on my skin dissolves me in into my seat. "Jace, stop. I'm going to be a Davenport in less than two hours." My hands go from trying to push him off, to bringing him closer. My mouth parts when his hand roams up to my thigh, bunching up my wedding dress. A part of me doesn't care if walk down the aisle with hickeys across my neck.

His hand grips my upper thigh tightly before he removes himself from me. "No, you're not. Want to know why, baby?"

"Why?" I moan.

"Because you're already a McAthy." He backs away from me, his crystal eyes shining and his lips flushed a bright pink.

"Who is McAthy? What are you talking about?"

He pulls out a piece of paper, folded nicely inside his suit, and puts it on the desk in front of me. I pick up the paper to read:

This license permits the couple to be married anywhere in the New York State only.

My heart starts beating faster the more I read. I stop, turning to Jace. He is not smiling, not laughing, just staring at me with tender eyes.

Spouse A: Jace McAthy
Spouse B: Lily Ballis

I turn the paper over to see our signatures and the license is stamped, dated, and officiated. This license was dated almost two weeks ago. I turn back to Jace to see his throat bob and his chest heave.

"I'm sorry. I couldn't let this wedding become official for you. I had to be the first." He gives me a small smile, his fists clenching at his sides.

I jump out of my seat, wrapping my arms around his neck. "And possibly the last," I cry.

"*Táim i ngrá leat.*"

More tears stream down my face as I chuckle into his suit. "I don't know what that means but thank you."

He kisses me on top of my head. "I better go. I have a wedding to fuck up." He takes the paper out of my hands, winking at me, and leaves me alone in the room.

Jace

I walk back into the church, finding Axel and Noah sitting next to each other. Mateo sits at the step of the stairs, talking on the phone. Most of the people here are his business partners, and they probably don't care one bit about this wedding.

I squeeze by a couple of people before sitting next to Noah.

"I'm surprised she didn't rip your head off," Noah says.

"Me too, honestly." I was nervous out of my mind that she was going to be pissed that I married her without her knowledge. If everything works in our favor, Mateo will get a call later tonight informing him that his marriage license with Lily has been denied due to her already being married. Rowan was able to find a marriage officiant willing to work with us and send our license to the City Clerk two weeks ago.

Rowan, Noah, and I worked our arses off to find out what is happening with all these women. The night of the yacht party, Rowan was able to identify all the Italian mafia members sitting in the cabin with Mateo. It didn't make sense why Mateo was doing business with them until we remembered what John had told us the night at the motel. When we finally put two and two together, I picked up Lily from the bridal shop, ready to make both of us disappear, but then she turned to me with her big green eyes and calmed me down. My strong, beautiful wife, ready to put herself in danger for others.

My. Wife.

Once Mateo realizes that this false wedding is already falsified, we will be on his heels, ready to take him down.

I stare at Mateo and he stares back at me. His head turns when the music starts playing and he stands from the stairs, putting his phone in his suit pocket. Everyone in the audience rises when the doors open, showing Lily standing in the archway. When I met her in the room, she was wearing a white wedding dress. But now, she stands there in a long, all-black dress. The front is cut deep, showing off her ivory chest, and her arms are covered in black lace. Her eyes roam around, looking at the hundreds of pairs of eyes staring at her, stopping when she meets mine. She grins and looks down at the floor before taking her first step down the aisle. We all sit down when Lily makes it to the stairs. I can see Mateo's jaw clench, but he extends his hand to help her up.

My ears buzz as the priest starts talking. By the time I come back to reality, they've finished their vows. Clenching my jaw so tight I wouldn't be surprised if my molars broke in half, the last words of the ceremony leave the priest's mouth, claiming them as husband and wife.

Mateo grabs Lily, dipping her down and kissing her. On autopilot, I stand, ready to put him six feet underground. My body jerks to the side as Noah grabs my arm and pulls me back down. I turn to look at Noah and Axel. Noah's eyes are strained on the front, clapping, and Axel laughs and shakes his head at me. When I turn my head to face the front, Mateo is shooting daggers at me with his eyes. I give him a big smile and slowly clap.

Chapter Thirty

Lily

♫ "Me and Your Mama (Mixed)" - Childish Gambino ♫

I have never cried so much in my entire life. Not when my parents told me they were proud of me for going to law school, not when I lost my teddy bear on a plane as a kid, not when I broke my arm on the playground. But for the past couple of months, I have been a constant sob. First it was when Jace asked me to marry Mateo, then when Celeste left me, then when Mateo proposed to me, again when Jace confessed his feelings, then when he told me we were married, and now, in front of this crowd of unknown people.

I ripped the white wedding dress off when Jace left the room. I couldn't let it signify a fresh start, a new journey with a new partner, pure and innocent. I only had a couple of weeks after I bought Mateo's wedding dress to create this silk black dress covered in black lace. Black can signify evil and darkness, which is what this wedding is. But I wanted to show the beauty in the color, the authority it can give you. The power it holds is an undeniable statement. And I needed to hold the power during the wedding. I wanted to feel in control of the situation.

I couldn't stop myself from finding Jace in the crowd, his eyes never leaving Mateo's as he smiles and claps his hands together, creating a sonic boom.

Play the part, Lily.

I grab Mateo's hand, smiling at him as we walk down the stairs and down the aisle. I keep my head down to avoid looking into bright blue eyes as we walk out of the church to the limousine that waits for us. Mateo opens the door for me to get in. I grab the bottom of my dress, stuffing it and me inside the vehicle. Out the window, I can see people starting to leave the church. I immediately spot Jace, Axel, and a younger looking guy who I assume is Noah. They quickly squeeze by people as they round the church, down an alley.

I turn toward Mateo to see him already texting on his phone. "Take us to the airport," he says into a microphone in limousine.

"Honeymoon already? I thought we planned a party after?" I smile at him, pretending to be fucking giddy about this whole situation, but in reality, my heart is pounding in my throat.

He turns to me, laying his phone in his lap. His bright brown eyes have turned into a void. Not an inch of his body moves, as if he doesn't need air to breathe. "You know, people talk a lot about the cat and mouse game."

There's only silence after his sentence. My smile falls as I stare back at him. I can feel the hair on the back of my neck stand. "Um, okay. What does that have to do with where we are going?" I force my lips to slightly curve again.

Play the part. He will find me.

"But people forget there is a more *dangerous* predator to the mouse than the cat." Mateo lifts his hands to his face as he turns to inspect his fingers like he just got a fresh manicure. "The venom is injected instantaneously into its prey and slowly, the poison weakens it until it succumbs." He laughs, his head falling back. "And can you believe they are looked down upon?! Seen as evil creatures?! Can something or someone truly be evil? Immoral and wicked? Or do we just do evil things?" The car becomes silent as he stares at me. "Who says what we do is fucking immoral?! Who made the rules of what is wicked?! What is morally wrong?!" He scoots closer to me, his hand reaching out and brushing a strand of hair that has fallen into my face. "What makes people so fucking evil, Lily?" His tongue darts out, licking his lips.

I say nothing as I push my hands under my thighs, sitting on top of them to stop them from shaking.

"You think you guys are so fucking clever, huh?" His hand still roams my face, outlining every feature of mine. "You think you guys are the cats in this game? Chasing the mouse?" He clicks his tongue against his teeth, moving his hand toward my throat while his eyes follow the movement. "The only thing you were chasing was your own demise."

I'm unable to swallow, the feeling of a cactus lodged against my throat. The dress is becoming too tight, the car too hot. His hand tightens around my throat when I reach for his arms, trying to take them off me. "Such a stupid bitch to trust those three idiots. They failed once. They will fail again."

My mouth pops open as I try to inhale.

"You better pray to a god that they deem you worthy. Because I sure as hell don't," he spits as his foot slams down onto mine.

A small cry falls from my lips, barely making a sound as my windpipe is constricted. Even with the heels I have on, I can feel the pain in my toes. Multiple tears fall down my face as I continue to claw at his arms and gasp for air. The more I scratch, the tighter his hand grips my throat. I let go of his arm and whip my palm across his face.

His head bends backward before he slowly turns to look back at me, laughing. "A fighter. Maybe they *will* deem you worthy. They love a fucking challenge." His tongue lashes out, licking away my tears from my cheeks. "I wonder who they will chose for you? Whoever it is, they don't get to have a piece of you until I have my share. I've waited too long for this. You've given yourself up to everyone, but you've refused me." He bares his teeth at me. "Me!"

My vision becomes blurry and there's a pounding in my ears.

"You'll have my child first before you give any to them." He finishes and slams his foot down on my other toes. He pulls my face closer to his, his lips brushing against my ear. "Welcome to the snake pit, baby."

Through my vision, I see his fist pull back, and hot searing pain hits my face before everything goes dark.

Chapter Thirty-One

Lily

I dart my tongue out, feeling the cracked skin on my lips and agonizing pain throughout my face. Something liquid runs past my eye off my cheek. My hands are bound behind my back, a shoulder lodged into my stomach, and my feet refuse to spread apart. I try to open my right eye, but a shooting pain stops me. I force my left eye open to see the ground below me, feet crunching against the rocks six feet below. The sound of a plane engine hums in the background.

"What do you mean it didn't go through?!"

I try to zone in on the voice yelling in the distance.

"How can she already be married?!"

I try to lift my head, my neck straining with the motion, and I swallow the bile that rises in my throat. I want to give him a big *fuck you* smile. I want to see his face when he realizes he has lost.

"Get her. She's fucking waking up."

A sharp pain flows through my neck and I try to fight to keep my eyes open, but they feel so heavy, and all I want to do is slee—

Chapter Thirty-Two

Lily

Hard, something solid. And cold. I can't feel my limbs, and I'm strapped down to something, immobilizing me. I open my one good eye, and my body starts to tremble. A plane? I'm on a plane.

"You told me I get first dibs!"

My head sways to the left, and I see Mateo's back to me.

"Fuck them! I want her first!"

There is only silence as he waits for the person on the other end of the line to respond.

"Fine... Fine. I will just go to Italy with her, and then I want her first." He hangs up the phone, turning toward me. "Fuck, you're a tough bitch, aren't you?" He stands above me, smiling as he watches me try to wriggle my way out. I hear something break, giving me more freedom to move, just in time for his hand to come down against my face once again.

Chapter Thirty-Three

Lily

My body flies into the air and crashes down on my right side. Discomfort darts through every limb of my body. I can't move even if I try to force myself. I can feel a breeze, with little droplets of water.

Water, god, I need water.

I try to swallow, to open my mouth. My lips feel glued shut with how dry they are. I try to force an eye open, but slam it shut when the sun sizzles my vision. My body bounces up again to land back on my right.

"Ugh, this bitch just doesn't quit."

I break my eye open, forcing my vision to clear. This time, it's no longer Mateo. Someone else is walking toward me. I look around to see we're on a boat and there's a built figure heading toward me with a needle in hand. I try to squirm away, finding myself stuck between seats. His hand pushes my face into the floor, and he injects the needle into the side of my neck.

Chapter Thirty-Four

Lily

I walk along the stone steps, surrounded by wildflowers. An open green field leads to a forest with tree branches reaching for the clear blue sky. The air smells of freshly cut grass mixed with wet dirt. Birds are in the distance, speaking to one another, a beautiful hum sung in the distance. I turn around to see a lake with a rowboat tied to the dock. I take in my surroundings, twirling at the sun kissing my skin. I make it to some steps that lead to the porch of a wooden house, vast white pillars holding the porch up. Two large windows are framed with shutters and there's a wooden front door.

I open the door to the house to see a black chamber with mannequins occupying every square inch. None of them are clothed and they have their backs to me. Clothes are scattered on the floor. Mirrors cover the walls. The abyss swallows the rest of the house. I take a step back when one of the mannequin's heads turns to face me, the other mannequin heads following. A pin drops in the distance and all of the mannequins' heads fall off their shoulders and roll onto the floor.

I turn to sprint back outside but find myself in another room instead. The once beautiful forest and open field have transformed into a sinister investigation room. I press my heels into the floor and look around, finding a chair in the middle, facing away from me. A figure appears in the chair with blonde hair and my breath hitches when a pair of blue eyes turns toward me.

Jace.

I run to him, but every step I take takes me further away. I can't reach him. He slowly continues to fade out of my sight. I try to scream, but no sound leaves my mouth. I reach my hands out to touch him, but with every move I make, the further he gets.

I wake up to tears running down my face. My body convulses as I try to calm my breathing. I'm no longer tied down. Lifting my hands, I run them along my face. Crimson flakes fall from my skin. A knot the size of a baseball has taken over my eye. My whole body feels mutilated, and my throat feels as if I have a thousand fires burning against my vocal cords. I turn my head side to side to see I'm in a concrete room with one door. I force my body up, bringing my knees to my chest.

He will find me.

He will find me.

My chest aches as I gasp for air. The wedding dress hangs off my body, torn to shreds. I have no shoes, and all my toes are bleeding.

Fuck.

I look at my big toe, trying to wipe off the blood to find the GPS chip. My nail polish has been removed, and there is no chip in sight.

"Fuck!" I yell.

The bolt on the door unlocks and it scrapes against the floor. A tray flies into the room, sending food onto the ground, including a cup of what I am assuming used to be water, but quickly evaporates into the concrete.

The drag of the door pierces my ears as it slams shut. I drag my body off the twin bed, crawling on my hands and knees. I pick up the tray, looking at my own reflection, and gasp at what I see of myself. I throw the tray at the door, letting out a broken scream.

He promised.

Chapter Thirty-Five

Jace

♫ "icantbelieveiletyougetaway" - aldn ♫

I stand behind Noah at Rowan's house, staring at the laptop. "What do you fucking mean you can't see her?!" Somehow, the little dot on the screen that was tracking Lily disappeared, stopping in the middle of New York somewhere.

"I don't know man, it just stopped," Noah says as he continues to type on his computer. I can hear the stress in his voice, but that doesn't stop my blood from running cold. I turn around, grabbing a vase, and throw it at the wall just so I don't knock Noah to the ground instead. The glass shatters, exploding everywhere.

"Hey!" Rowan comes flying down the stairs, grabbing me by my shoulders and pushing me against the wall. "The fuck is the matter with you? Keep it down," he hisses between his teeth.

"We lost Lily," I growl.

"What do you mean you *lost* Lily?" Celeste questions as she comes wobbling down the stairs, her belly slightly protruding from her shirt.

I clench my hands, fucking ready to put myself six feet in the dirt for waking her up. The pregnancy has been hard on both Rowan and Celeste, with her complications making her bedridden.

Rowan turns to me with flames dancing in his eyes, I can assume for waking Celeste up and for slipping up in front of her since she still knows nothing about what is going on.

"I better have an answer before I hit the last step. I don't want to be walking down these stairs for no reason."

Rowan lets me go, running to Celeste. I turn around, my hands pounding against my head. Noah is leaning back on the couch, his hands pulling at his hair as he continues to stare at the computer.

"Heaven, baby, go back to bed," Rowan orders as he continues to try and guide her back up the stairs.

"No. What is going on? I want to know right now," Celeste demands when she hits the last step, looking at all three of us.

"Lily got married to Mateo to help us try and find out where Mateo is selling women, and we made this whole plan and installed a GPS in Lily, but now the GPS is gone, and we have no idea where she is," Noah spits out all the details like someone is holding a gun to his head.

"Feckin' *bollocks*," I whisper, turning around and pacing at the front door, ready to dash before Rowan grabs a gun.

"I'm going to kill you," Rowan points to Noah, and stomps to the couch where he sits. Noah stands, and they both start acting like athletes, trying to see who can get around the other first.

"She needed to know!" Noah yells.

"She is carrying my fucking baby! She doesn't need this stress!" Rowan yells as they both run around the couch.

I stop pacing around the door and turn toward Celeste as she looks at me with tears in her eyes.

"I promised I would find her," I whisper. Only Celeste can hear me as Rowan and Noah continue to yell at each other.

"Stop," Celeste says, but Rowan finally has gotten ahold of Noah, grabbing him and putting him in a chokehold. "I said stop!" she screams.

Everything in the house freezes. Rowan and Noah don't move. The AC stops blowing, the ceiling fan slowing down, yet the air gets colder by the second.

"Now—" Celeste starts, walking toward the couch. Rowan throws Noah off him, jumping up to grab ahold of Celeste. "Don't you fucking dare touch me," she seethes, pointing her finger in Rowan's face. I can see the life fall from his eyes as he stares at her and backs away.

"Now, we are going to stop acting like little children and figure out how to find my best friend. Everyone sit the fuck down and hand me the laptop."

Noah rushes to sit next to Celeste and I take her other side as Rowan steadily sits on the chair next to the couch.

"I swear to god, if anything happens to her, all of your heads will be put into a box for decorations."

Four hours later, we finally have a plan. Celeste helped us get our heads out of our arses and settle down to think about what happened. We have Lily's last pinned location, and we know what kind of car she left in after the wedding. We were able to look at street cameras and follow the car's location to the airport. There was only one private plane that left the airstrip around 5:45 p.m., and it was scheduled to land in Dubois, Wyoming.

"Do you really think they are in Wyoming?" Rowan asks as he packs a suitcase filled with medical supplies for Celeste—because of course she is coming and there was no way he was able to plead her out of it. I think, in the back of his mind, he is glad she is coming, because if something were to happen to her while he was not home, his world would crash into a million pieces.

Noah is downstairs, packing *other* supplies, and I can't gather myself enough to drive through New York to pack for myself. We have a six-hour flight from New York to Wyoming and I'd rather not waste another second.

I sit on the bed, staring at my hands. "It's better than us sitting here not knowing."

Noah enters the room, dropping three duffle bags. "I've got everything. The rifles, the subs, the pumps—" Noah shuts his mouth when Celeste enters the room, towel drying her hair.

"No need to stop now. It's not like I don't know my boyfriend and his friends like to murder people."

Rowan walks over to her, kissing her on the temple. My chest constricts as I watch my best friend not only fall in love, but start his family—something I've only dreamed about, and if I don't find Lily, I may never watch that dream come true.

We all pack into Rowan's new half-a-million-dollar SUV. He says it's his "dad car," but I can't wait for the little kid to pop out and throw their juice boxes all over these white leather seats.

Seven hours later, we land on an empty runway. I jump out of Rowan's private jet first, noticing the wooden sign that says, *Welcome to Dubois, Wyoming*—nothing but mountains covered in snow.

I walk to the triangle-shaped building and burst through the door. I'm met with an empty front desk and a sign that says, *Ring Bell*. I slam my hand on it once.

Twice.

Three times, before some old man finally cuts around the corner. "Can I help you?"

Rowan, Celeste, and Noah all come inside. The old man walks with a cane and has a head full of grey hair. He stares at us like we are from another planet.

"I need information about a plane that landed last night." My hands grab his desk as I look between him and his computer.

"No can do, kiddo. No information leaves these buildings unless it's your own info, my boy." The man waddles behind his desk, throwing his cane on top of it.

My fingers crack from my forceful grip on the old oak.

"Listen, sir," Celeste comes wobbling up, holding her stomach. Her hand lands on my back, trying to ease the tension pulsing through me. She peeks at the nametag placed on top of his desk. "Mr. Buford, we really need some information, it's an emergency."

The old man grabs his cane, pointing it in Celeste's face. "Like I said, lady, no info leaves this premises."

Rowan comes up behind Celeste, using his finger to slowly remove the cane from her face. "Don't do that."

"I don't know who you hooligans are, or where you come from. Or even how you landed on my runway, but y'all better leave before I call the cops."

I can hear Noah in the back mumble, "fucking idiot," before he heads outside and comes back in a second later, dropping all three duffle bags on the floor. Rowan and I turn our heads toward each other, ready to get the job done how we usually do it.

That's until Celeste grabs both of our arms as we are turning away. She takes one long breath and gives the man a wide smile. "Mr. Buford, I don't know how you guys do it here in Wyoming, but we are from New York, and we like to get shit done. So, you will either tell me about this fucking plane! Or my boyfriend and his friends are going to open those bags behind us, and I promise you're not going to like what you see." Celeste's voice ends in a whisper.

We all stare at her shocked, as we have never seen her so sweaty and frustrated.

Mr. Buford stands from his chair, eyeing Celeste up and down. "You pregnant? Who let her fly in her condition? Y'all should be ashamed of yourselves."

Rowan pulls his arm out of Celeste's grip, heading straight for Noah, who is already bent down, opening the bags.

"You do not get to tell me what I can and cannot do in my fucking condition! You old fucking dickwad! I swear to god, if you do not tell me who the fuck came out of that plane last night, I will put a bullet through your head, dig the bullet out of your skull, then save it for my baby as a gift for when they are born! I am losing my patience, it's hot as fuck in this building, and my bladder feels like it's lodged in my ribs. So I swear, *Mr. Buford*, you have ten seconds to start talking!"

My mouth curls up as I watch Celeste hold her fingers up, counting down from ten. She is going to be a great mom.

Rowan comes to stand beside her, cocking the gun near his leg, behind the desk. The old man's eyes dart between all four of us standing in front of him. By the time Celeste hits eight, Rowan holds up the shotgun, pointing.

"Okay, okay, my god. I'll pull up video footage."

Rowan and I go to stand behind him, watching him pull up footage of last night. Three men get out of a plane, one holding Lily over his shoulder.

"Give me your fucking keys." I hold out my hand to Buford.

"W-What but I—"

"Give me your fucking keys!"

His hand trembles as he reaches into his pocket, pulling out a set of keys. As soon as they hit my hand, I dash for the front door. Noah is already heading in the opposite direction after Rowan called him over to get a copy of the footage.

I push open the door, hitting the lock button on the keys to hear an old minivan alarm go off. As soon as I reach the car, I rip off the license plate. "Fuck!" The license plate flies out of my hand, somewhere off in the distance. Opening the front door, I bend down, pulling out my pocketknife, and start scratching at the VIN number.

"I was able to get the car information from the video footage."

I turn around to see Noah behind me, holding his laptop.

"Last seen location was at the port of South Beach."

"South Beach what?" I grit through my teeth, my palm squeezing at the blade in my hand.

"South Beach... Oregon."

I stand to my full height, turning away from Noah, and chuck the car keys into the crystal snow.

Chapter Thirty-Six

Lily

I no longer know what time it is, what day it is, where I am, or who I'm with. A pile of food sits in a corner as they continue trying to feed me. I gathered all the plastic forks they have thrown with the food, breaking off the ends of them, and with every moment I have, I've sharpened the ends through a hole in the concrete wall. It's not as sharp as a knife, not as sturdy as a knife, but putting multiple together, tied with the fabric I ripped from my dress should, maybe, work.

I squat to the left of the door, on the floor, waiting for my next meal, waiting for them to open the door so I can try to make my escape. Because now, only I can save myself. It's too late. My GPS chip is gone, and it has been too many days. I was lost the second his foot slammed onto mine. My mind rushes back to the picture I have implanted in my brain of Mateo smiling down at me as his fingers closed around my neck. Tears prickle in my eyes. I should have called Celeste. I should have told her everything.

"Such a stupid bitch to trust those three idiots."

"If no one can save me, I will save myself," I whisper.

"If no one can save me. I will. Save. Myself."

My body freezes as I hear the bolts unlock. A set of legs come into view. I swing my hand in the air, my homemade knife gripped tightly between my fingers, swinging right at the Achilles tendon. The knife's head breaks off, barely slicing through his skin.

"Fuck! You fucking bitch."

Not enough. It wasn't enough.

I lean my head back, forcing myself to look up. The food from the tray is thrown behind the man's shoulder before he swings the metal up and brings it back down to slam it on my face. I swiftly move before it hits me, crawling around him. I force my body to rise, standing in the hallway. I look around to see multiple doors lining the wall with men standing at each one.

I am completely surrounded.

My body makes a three-sixty as I try to find somewhere, anywhere, to go. I dart toward the end of the hall, my feet moving on their own, but I don't make it two steps before a man comes up behind me, grabs me, and throws me over his shoulders. I scream until my lungs feel like they could fall out of my mouth, kicking at his back and clawing at his stomach. We walk in the opposite direction, passing the room I was just in.

He throws me off his shoulders into another room. My head hits the floor, bouncing. White lights shatter my vision, and I feel a sharp pain shoot through my neck. I open my mouth to try to inhale. My eyes burn and tears fall down my face. I stare at the ceiling as I continue to gasp, my lungs begging for air.

I'm grabbed by one of my arms, my body pulled into the air as they rip off the rest of my dress. One of my legs is lifted, the other following as they pull the black fabric down my body. My ringing ears can't decipher if the screams are coming from me or from others around. Three men hold me up as my body keeps falling, my knees buckling. One arm is wrapped around my chest, forcing me to stand straight. A man in front of me unbuckles a white coat before putting it on my body. The man behind me wraps the ties around my back, forcing my arms to hug myself, and finishes it off with the zipper and buckles.

The arm around me releases, letting my body go and my head hits the cement floor for a third time. My shoulders take most of the fall, notably the one that has been stinging with pain for the past couple of days.

I watch as eight pairs of shoes leave the room, shutting the door behind them, and leave me on the cold cement with nothing on except the straitjacket.

Chapter Thirty-Seven

Jace

♫ "listen before i go" - Billie Eilish ♫

I stare out into the distance as the blur of trees pass by. Only the whistle of the wind fills the silence through the rolled-down window. I sit in the back seat with Noah. Rowan is driving and Celeste is in the passenger seat. It took us three hours to fly from Wyoming to North Bend, Oregon. On the flight, Noah was able to find footage of Lily dragged onto a boat with three other men. Someone had recorded it on their phone and posted it to their private social media.

No police report was filed.

That boat then left South Beach, and fucking docked at Vancouver Island. Fucking Canada. They took her to fucking Canada.

I bring my face closer to the window, letting the wind strike me until I can't inhale. Until the icy breeze wraps around my lungs and chokes me from the inside. I let them burn for as long as I can until I feel nothing but pain. I don't want to feel anything but the pain I inflict upon myself because it is what I deserve. I no longer deserve to live this life for what I have done. I deserve to have my head placed on a fucking stick and lit on fire with a thousand lighters. She didn't deserve this.

She doesn't deserve this.

This was not how it was supposed to go.

I don't deserve her. But I can't live a life without her.

I turn my head away once it feels like my lungs are going to collapse, leaning my forehead onto the back of Celeste's seat.

"We will find her," Noah says quietly.

If there is no longer a Lily, there is no longer me. She has had her fingers wrapped around my heart for years and without the warmth of her fingers, my heart will no longer beat.

"You know, one time, Lily and I were at a dive bar, and they started playing 'Toxic' by Brittany Spears. Lily was so drunk that she stood on a chair and started dancing." Celeste lets out a little laugh. "She was wearing these six-inch heels and some dress she sewed up the same night. The chair leg ended up breaking from under her and she fell backward, ripped her dress and hit her head. Blood started gushing everywhere." Celeste turns around in her seat, grabbing my hand. "I freaked out of course, because she was bleeding, but she started to laugh so hard. Her dress had ripped down her ass and she was worried someone was going to see, but she was so drunk she didn't notice we were the only people in the bar." I feel Celeste's hand squeeze mine. "Jace."

I turn my head to see her staring at me. "She is strong. She is going to be okay," she says.

"What if—What if I am too late? What if I took too long? I promised her I would be right there, but it has been days. I know she is strong, but what if she wants nothing to do with me after? I put her through this. I put this trauma upon her." I swallow the thickness in my throat.

"You waited years to talk to her. Now is your time to fight for her."

Chapter Thirty-Eight

Lily

♫ "Carry Me Home (feat. Maverick Sabre)" - Jorja Smith ♫

I open my eyes, feeling my head throbbing. There are three trays placed near my head filled with food I wouldn't even feed a dog. I roll my body along the floor like a kid rolling down a hill till I hit a wall. I lean my body against it, pulling myself into a sitting position before I stand up fully.

Every muscle in my body aches. I look down to see my legs covered in dirt, blood, bruises, and scratches. I look around the room to find nothing but the four walls surrounding me. I pace around, trying to think of a new plan and how to get out of this straitjacket.

I stop pacing when the door open and a man in a suit walks in. Something about him looks so familiar.

"No hard feelings about all that..." His fingers swirl in the air, pointing to my body. "Right?"

I don't say anything, watching as he puts his hands in the front pockets of his slacks. He takes two more steps toward me, and I back into the wall behind me.

"If it wasn't for my wife, this whole set-up would have never had to happen." He sighs.

Where have I seen him before?

My body falls to the floor when I hear a girl scream following a gun shot.

Then another.

And another.

"Son of a bitch." The man who is standing in front of me runs out the door, closing it behind him.

I stay on the floor, hearing multiple shots fired in the hallway. The door to my room opens, and a guy flings himself in, closing the door behind him as he looks out the little window.

"What is going on?" I'm able to spit out.

He turns around, looking at me from head to toe. "Shut up, bitch," he snarls before turning back around. I notice the rip in his jeans near the bottom of his leg. This is the man I tried to slice. I spot the gun he is holding in his hand, along with the one wrapped around his body.

Three more gunshots echo in the hallway. I push my body deeper into the wall, wishing I could sink in and disappear. The gunshots get closer each minute. When the man reaches for the door handle, the tiny glass window he was peeping out of shatters in his face. I slam my eyes closed, my body tensing, and prepare for the bullet to hit my skin.

When I feel no additional inflicted pain, I open my eyes to see the man gradually fall back like a tree being cut down. The door swings open and another man in a balaclava, vest, and all-black outfit stands in the hallway.

"In here!"

The guy standing in the door is pushed away and another man in the same getup, comes striding toward me. I wriggle my arms, trying to break free. I can't be kidnapped again. I can't disappear with more strangers again.

They will never find me.

I watch as he steps on the chest of the man on the floor, making blood gush even more. I shut my eyes, my breathing becoming heavy and my head spinning.

"*Álainn.*" Cold hands grab my cheeks, twisting my head. "I'm so sorry, baby. Can you open your eyes for me?"

I keep my eyes closed, tears running down my face.

"Fuck, Lily, please open your eyes."

I inhale a deep breath, opening my eyes to see two clear blue ones staring at me, and I crack. I shatter as if I were a falling star entering the atmosphere. A cry rips from my mouth, my knees buckle, but I am caught in his hands.

"Lily, I am so sorry. I am so sorry."

We fall to the floor, my back pressed against his chest, my body between his legs. I can feel him unbuckling the jacket, but just as he is about to slide it down my shoulders, he stops. His hand runs along my skin. "Fuck," he whispers.

"P-please, please. Can we just leave?" I choke out. I know what he is looking at. I can feel it. The bruises. They hurt. Everything hurts.

"No. You're not walking out of here with any piece of this place with you." His body slowly leaves mine. I turn around to see him walk to the door and close it. He grabs the dead man on the floor by the legs and drags him into the corner. Jace removes his mask, his golden blonde hair scattered, sweaty, and messy along his forehead. His hand reaches for his belt, unbuckling it and pulling his pants down. He walks over to me, bending down, and slowly lifts my legs to step into his pants, pulling them up to cover my naked lower body. He takes out a pocketknife, creating a new hole in the belt before securing it to my waist.

His arms reach for the jacket, sliding it off my shoulders. I close my eyes, slamming my mouth shut to avoid a whimper. My shoulders are crying in agony.

He takes off his vest and shirt. This time, I can't keep my mouth shut. I hiss when he slowly lifts my arms above my head to put his shirt over me.

"I'm so sorry." Tears form in his eyes as he stares at me, dressed in his oversized T-shirt and baggy cargo pants. He grabs the hem of his shirt, ripping it. "Place your arm right here." He grabs my hand and demonstrates. I keep it there while he makes a sling for my shoulder. He reaches his hand out to me, standing in front of me in nothing but his boxers, socks, and shoes. I let my hand slowly gravitate to his like the magnets we are.

Holding my hand, he bends down and picks me up to carry me out the door. When we leave the room, I look over his shoulder to see Rowan at the end of the hall, pinning someone against a wall with a gun pointed at their head. Another man, probably Noah, comes out of a room with a large knife, wiping the blood off onto his jeans. I bury my head into Jace's neck when Rowan pulls the trigger.

Jace kicks down the door in front of him. The sun burns on my exposed skin, a salty breeze mixed with wet dirt invading my nose. I'm placed inside a SUV, the door shutting behind me.

"Why didn't you fucking tell me?!"

I turn to see Celeste staring at me with tears falling down her face. My mouth falls open and I let out a scream as I cry into my hands.

I wake up to the sound of the trunk behind me opening. I don't know when I fell asleep, or how long I have been asleep for. I turn around to see Jace, Rowan, and Noah, putting bags into the trunk. All three of them are covered in blood from their face down to their hands.

"We have to go before the cops come," Rowan says.

I turn to the front of the car. Through the window, I see multiple girls standing in front of the building. Some of them look familiar from the yacht party. They huddle close together, wearing bloody, baggy clothing. Jace walks up to them, saying something before they all head back inside.

The back passenger door opens, Noah throwing himself in the seat next to me. He has bright hazel eyes and dark brown curly hair. He looks at me, smiling, showing his one dimple. "Hi, I'm Noah." He holds out his hand covered in blood.

I look, but my gaze snaps away when Celeste sighs and shakes her head. Both the driver's door and the other passenger-side door open, and Rowan gets in to drive. Jace sits next to me.

"How you feeling?" Jace looks at me with his eyebrows pinched.

"Where are we?"

"Fucking Canada," Noah snaps. "Hey, actually, can we go see Niagara Falls?"

"No," both Rowan and Celeste say simultaneously.

"Jesus, Noah, really? Now is not the time," Rowan says.

Celeste turns around in her seat. "There is one in New York. Go see that one when we're back home."

"But the one in Canada looks cooler," Noah whispers, turning his head to look out the window.

"We have to stop somewhere to get cleaned up." Jace leans over me, talking to Celeste and Rowan up front.

"Can we get a hotel? I'm fucking beat," Noah yawns, his hand softly punching at the top of the car roof.

Rowan turns to Celeste, looking at her. "Yeah, I think that may be best." He grabs Celeste's hand from across the seat, picking it up and kissing it.

Chapter Thirty-Nine

Lily

♫ "Running Up That Hill (A Deal With God) [Piano Version]" - Henry Smith ♫

My body jolts when I feel the car stop. I lift my head off Jace's shoulder and turn to see him staring at me. On my left, Noah is snoring with his legs spread apart, pushing more of my body onto Jace.

Celeste turns around in her seat, looking at all of us. "I think it would be safer if I go get the keys since all of you look... like that."

"Come back here if they give you a hard time," Rowan states.

Celeste pats on Rowan's shoulder before opening the car door and jumping out. I watch her as she passes by the front windshield, her hand holding her stomach—

"What the fuck?!" I scream, leaning forward to try and get a better look before she heads inside. "Is she pregnant?!" I crawl over Noah with one hand and just as I'm about to open the car door, I hear it lock.

"I'd rather you not run inside looking like you have been kidnapped," Rowan says, eyeing me through the review mirror.

"I *was* kidnapped," I snap.

"Is it kidnapping if you knew it was coming?" My head turns toward Noah, smiling at me, his eyes roaming down to where my hand is planted near his crotch.

My body is pulled backward into Jace as he holds onto my hips. His lips press on the top of my head as he hums into my hair. It reminds me of when I first heard him make that noise. What it makes me feel. How he makes me feel. I let my body relax into him, melt into him as he holds me tight, and I feel safe again. Like everything else doesn't matter. Everything that happened these past couple of days doesn't matter.

Because I'm safe again.

Safe with him.

When Celeste gets back, she opens the car door, holding two pairs of keys in the air. "That is all they had left."

Her voice snaps me out of my comfort and I remember we are not alone. "You didn't fucking tell me!" I yell at her from the back of the car.

"Baby, stop yelling. I'm sure you have a concussion," Jace whispers into the side of my face.

"And you didn't fucking tell me!" Celeste yells back at me.

Everything becomes quiet as we stare at each other between the seats.

Until Noah whistles. "Anyway, I call a room to myself, so couples—"

"No," Rowan, Celeste, Jace, and I all say in unison.

"I feel like this is a really fucked-up version of the show *New Girl*. Have y'all seen it?" Noah questions as he opens the car door, pulling out a pack of cigarettes and hitting them on the back of his hand.

Rowan sighs from the front seat. "Noah can stay with us." Celeste tosses Jace a set of keys. He opens the door, extending his hand to help me out of the car. I wince when I step out into the light.

We walk into our motel room that smells like mildew and dust. "Where are we now?" I ask as Jace sits down on one of the beds.

"Jewell, Oregon. I think."

I nod as I look around the room.

"Lily, I am so sorry." He walks fast toward me but stops only inches away.

My head falls down to look at the floor, my fingers grasping onto his shirt I'm still wearing and twirling it between my fingers until his hand reaches out to cover mine.

"I should have had multiple plans for you. I should have done more than the tracker. Doing the marriage certificate—" He shakes his head. "I knew he would end up pushing the plans, but I didn't think he knew about the GPS. As soon as we get home, you can file for the divorce. I just—"

"Is that what you want?" I ask, looking up at him. He is silent for a moment as I watch his eyes pierce through mine.

"No."

I nod, looking around and trying to not let the tears fall from my eyes. His cold fingertips touch my chin, forcing me to look at him.

"I agreed to this. I knew what I was getting myself into. I saw all the girls we saved and I-I think it was worth it. I'm safe now." I look at his face, at the crimson splatters enhancing his blue eyes. He leans in closer, cutting off the air between us. I close the gap and let my lips embrace his. His arms wrap lightly around my body, pulling me closer to him. I let the electricity flow through my skin, bringing me back to life.

We may have never had an official wedding, but I would marry him again and again if it meant I could kiss him every day. Jace is mine. He always has been, always will be.

♫ "Nothing Sweeter" – Naomi Sharon ♫

I wrap the towel around my head as my arm muscles pull tight at every movement. I don't think my shoulder is broken, probably just severely bruised. I took off the handmade sling Jace made for me before I got in the shower and let the hot steam soothe my muscles. When I got out of the shower, I saw all the bruises along my body. From my face down to my legs. Noah dropped off clothes for everyone he bought from a local store nearby. I throw on a black T-shirt that says *Oregon* with mountains in the background and a pair of pink striped athletic shorts. Jace lies on the bed, flipping through channels on the television. His arm rests behind his head, making his bicep bulge. He's only wearing boxers, showing off his abs.

"Are you sure you're okay? Do you think maybe we should see a doctor? Get you checked out?" he asks hesitantly, setting down the remote. He stares at me like I might vanish into this floor right in front of him. "I'm scared that—" He bangs his head against the headboard, his hands covering his face.

I walk toward him, swinging my legs over to straddle his lap. I slowly rip his hands away from his face. "I'm okay Jace. I wasn't touched like *that*, if that is what you're scared about. I'm here. I'm alive. Yes, I might need a little therapy and yeah, I was worried that you wouldn't find me—"

"Fuck," he growls, placing his hands over his face again.

I quickly swipe his hands away. "But you did. You came for me."

"I would tear this whole world to shreds to find you, Lily. I would never give up. I would do unimaginable things to people to find you."

"I know." I place a soft kiss on his lips.

Both our heads turn to the door when we hear three knocks. Jace gets out of bed, grabbing the gun on the nightstand, and hides it behind his back. When he opens the door, Celeste is standing outside with bags of food.

She looks between us. "Can we have a moment?"

Jace turns toward me, nodding before walking out the door.

Celeste walks in, closing the door behind her. "It may not be my cooking, but—"

"I'm sorry I didn't tell you," I cut her off.

"I'm sorry I didn't tell you," she says, holding out her arms.

Oh god, a Celeste hug. I must have never left that building. I died and now I'm in heaven. I run to hug her, but then stop, backing up and placing my hand on her stomach to feel.

"It's been hard." Celeste's hand covers mine on her belly. She is already pretty petite, so it's not hard to tell there is a little baby in there. "I found out late that I was pregnant. I'll be seventeen weeks tomorrow. This is my first time leaving the house since finding out. That is why no one knew I was scared that—"

"I'm sorry I haven't called. And I'm sorry I didn't tell you," I say softly.

"I'm sorry too."

Celeste waddles away to sit down on the bed and pull out the food from the bags. "Congratulations, by the way."

I stand there, staring at her.

"You're married." She smiles at me. "I guess you were right. First comes baby." She points to herself. "Then comes marriage." She points at me.

We both snort out a laugh while I sit on the bed, picking out the burgers from the bag.

Both are bodies jump when the front door swings wide open. Three men, all over six feet tall, stand in the doorway. Rowan and Jace are upfront, Noah behind them.

"Sharing is fucking caring," Noah says, pushing between Rowan and Jace. He jumps onto the bed and grabs a burger.

"Save one for Celeste, she needs to eat for two." Rowan comes striding in after Noah, grabbing him by the collar of his shirt.

Jace shrugs his shoulder, closing the door behind him. He walks toward me, picking me up so he can seat himself on the bed with me sitting in his lap.

Tears start streaming down my face as I watch the three large men and my pregnant best friend all squeeze onto one twin bed, snatching food from out of each other hands.

We may be across the country, in a disgusting motel, but everything feels right. I was broken, beaten, and bruised. But everyone surrounding me, at this moment, right here, they're ready to pick up my broken pieces.

They were never going to give up until I was safe in all their arms. Putting my life at risk for the women I saw outside that building will never be something I will regret.

Everything that has happened can't be changed or forgotten, so I will never regret what I have done. I will never regret giving my love to the one who has loved me since day one.

EPILOGUE

Lily

One Year Later...

"Can I open my eyes now?" I squeeze my hand tighter around Jace's fingers as he drags me out of the car into the streets of New York.

"Just a second."

I hear a bell ring above my head. Jace grabs my hips and moves me a little to the left. "Okay, now open."

My eyes adjust as the lights turn on.

"Surprise!"

I look around the room to see Rowan and Celeste. Celeste is carrying Alec, my precious nephew, and I also spot Noah, Axel, and—my mom, my dad, and all my siblings.

I turn to my side to see Jace smiling, showing off his perfect, sharp white teeth, his blue eyes sparkling in the light. I look around more at the room, at the random shelves, boxes, wood, and trash scattered all along the floor.

Jace walks behind me, grabbing me by the hips, and brushes his lips against my ear. "It used to be my father's hardware store. I know it still needs to be cleaned up, but it's a start," he whispers into my ear.

"What—What is it for?" I ask.

He slips his arm around me, holding an envelope in his hand labeled *The New School*. "I figured you would need more space for your designs—"

I snatch it from his hand, tearing it open. Reading it to myself, my hand covers my mouth, and tears form in my eyes. I can hear party blowers and cheers from all my siblings.

When we got back to New York after I was kidnapped, I dropped out of law school and called my parents. I told them I couldn't do it any longer. That I wanted to be a fashion designer. Jace was there at my side to give me courage. They weren't even close to being upset. Well, they were upset I waited so long to tell them—but once I showed them my drawings, they did the same thing they did when they found out I was going to college for law school. They jumped up and down, chanting.

"I got in!" I scream, the party blowers and cheers continuing from everyone. I start jumping up and down, twirling and throwing my hands in the air, but stop when I open my eyes to see Jace on one knee behind me, the room falling silent.

"Lily McAthy... *mo ghrá, a chuisle mo chroí, my anam cara, mo mhuirnín dílis.*"

"What is he saying?" my father asks in the background.

"Shush!" Celeste whispers to him.

"I didn't do it right the first time, I won't let there be a next. It's you and me until our world is no longer. It's you and me until our last breaths. I would choose you today, tomorrow, in a thousand lifetimes, in a thousand worlds. God, Lily, I would choose you. I do choose you. Do you choose me?" He reaches into his pocket, pulling out a box and opening it to show an oval-cut sapphire ring surrounded by other little diamonds.

"Hurry up and says yes. I'm starving over here!" Noah yells from behind me.

"God, you guys are the worst," Celeste whispers.

"Today, tomorrow, and forever," I cry.

I watch as Jace puts the ring on my finger. Standing, he picks me up and spins me around.

"I love you, Lily McAthy," he whispers into my ear.

"I love you, Jace McAthy."

BONUS SCENE

Rowan

Jace jumps out the vehicle, running to the trunk of the SUV and pulling out all our bags. I open one and start handing the rifles to Jace and Noah. Jace pulls out three bulletproof vests, each of us putting them on. Noah pulls out his machete, twirling it in the sunlight. Once we are all set, we look at each other, nodding.

Jace slams the trunk shut and I run to Celeste's door, swinging it open.

"Not this again." She rolls her eyes when I put the Glock in her lap.

I give her a kiss on the forehead, closing her passenger door, and walk up to stand next to Jace and Noah. The warehouse reminds me of a shipment container. One exit on each end, with the unknown inside. We all nod to each other, pulling down our masks. Jace swings the door open, heading in first, finger pulling the trigger. I'm right behind him, shooting every man in sight above Jace's shoulder. The long hallway has doors inches from each other. Noah behind us, starts opening them, women screaming at the sight of him.

A man tackles me from my left, coming out of one of the rooms. I slam the end of my gun into his head, flipping it around and pulling the trigger at his side temple. Standing, I feel eyes on the back of my head. Turning around, I can see a man in a window, and within seconds, I lift my gun and shoot.

I turn to my right, seeing Noah slash the neck of a guy he's wrestling with. "Noah, cover Jace ahead! They are hiding in the rooms!"

"No shit!" He stands, running past me.

The outside of the warehouse looked fucking small, but as soon as we stepped in, it was larger than we expected, and we did not expect this many men hiding in one spot.

I swing the door open in front of me to make sure the man I shot through the window is dead and to double-check none of his friends are in here. I see a red river flowing on the floor. When I drag my eyes up, I see Lily sitting in the corner, naked, with a straitjacket wrapped around her. "In here!" I scream at Jace. He turns his head to me, stepping on every man who has fallen, pushing me to the side, his eyes finding Lily.

I walk away from the door, giving them privacy. At the end of the hall, Noah is making his way through every room, swinging his knife around like a gladiator. He stands on top of a man, slamming the machete into the victim's forehead. A man pops out of a room wearing a suit, and dashes toward the back exit. Noah pulls out a blade from his pants and sends it flying through the air, striking the man on the back of his knee. The man wails, falling to the floor.

Noah makes it to the man, grabbing him by the collar of his suit jacket, machete pinned to his neck.

"Wait!" I scream.

I walk toward them and come face to face with the one and only Lancer Harper. I push Noah to the side, picking Lance up by the neck, and slam his head against the wall. I place my arm on his neck to pin him there.

"Well, if it isn't father of the year," I say in his face.

"Oh shit," Noah whispers. I can hear his boots crunch on broken glass as he walks away.

Lance tries to speak, but when he opens his mouth, I press my arm against his Adam's apple harder.

"No need to speak, Lance. You had your chance a long time ago." I press the muzzle of my gun into his forehead. "I would say you're lucky Jace didn't let me kill you that night. But..." I turn my head, looking. Noah is dragging bodies out into the hallway, piling them up. "I think this might be a misfortune for you. Losing your men. Losing… as always." I stare into his eyes, easing off his neck a little because a part of me would like to hear what he has to say.

Using my hand that is holding the gun, I pull my mask up and over my head, quickly pointing my weapon back at him.

As soon as he opens his mouth, I pull the trigger. I changed my mind. I don't want to hear his lies, excuses, or manipulating words about why he is trafficking woman to Italy. I release the grip I have on his neck, letting his body slide to the ground. I back away a few steps before I pull the trigger two more times, hitting his chest and stomach.

"I'm going to buy you a trophy that says, *My Favorite Son*," Noah says as he comes to stand beside me.

"Do you ever shut the fuck up?" I pat down my lifeless father, finding a burner phone in his pocket and a medallion ring that looked similar to the one John had. I look around at all the bodies on the floor. "Where is Mateo?"

"Not here."

"What do you mean, not here?!" I start walking down the hallway, scanning the faces of the dead bodies, trying to find that fucker. I turn to Noah. He stands behind me, covered in more blood than any of us.

"Why are you looking at me like that?" he asks.

"He said this wasn't over." I laugh maniacally, walking toward the exit of the building. "I'm going to kill both of those bastards."